The Well

Revealing the Hidden Nature of Reality

Lilly Andaman

For
Mitch, Richie and Grace ... the stars in my Universe

CONTENTS

"Is not the quest for reality in a world of illusions the task for which each comes into the world?"

Manly P. Hall

.

CHAPTER 1

Empire, Michigan
21st December 2012

The thought of her mother's words emerged clearly into her mind, as if she were standing there whispering into her ear at that very moment. She turned her head ever so slightly, acknowledging an eerie presence.

"Lilly" she said, "The hardest thing about life is living it. The rest is easy."

At the time, as an eight-year-old she didn't really understand what she meant. But now, at this moment 20 years on, she understood perfectly well. In fact, it seemed a silent prophecy.

Lilly returned her focus to the bathroom basin and the flow of blood winding its way in a circular motion towards the abyss of the plug-hole. It mesmerised her. The elixir of her life being offered from the chalice of her body; a sacrifice; a gesture of her surrender to the overwhelming despair that had engulfed her being. The sign of the cross, engraved deeply within the pink flesh of her wrist, was now a visible symbol of the ultimate abandonment by that of her God.

She felt no pain despite the deepness of the wound. Physical pain had been obliterated by the constant emotional numbness that she had felt for months. The release of her blood provided a temporary relief, even if only for minutes until it congealed and ceased to flow; a sign of her body's innate wisdom to ensure the preservation of her life, despite her deep longing to the contrary.

Lilly placed the blade gently on the edge of the basin, satisfied that the task was complete. She opened the bathroom cabinet in front of her to retrieve a bandage to swathe her bloodied wrist. The multiple bottles and coloured packets of medication stared back at her; their promise of lifting the dark cloud of despair that was her constant shadow had remained unfulfilled. Nothing seemed to help. But then, how do you heal a broken heart, she thought.

She took the soft white bandage from the shelf and closed the cabinet door. The mirror on the cabinet provided a brief opportunity to catch a glimpse of her reflection, as her tired brown eyes stared back at her, moist from tears. Her long, brown hair draped to her shoulders, enjoying the freedom from her usual style of wearing it up. Even without make-up, the features of her face exuded a natural beauty. Her sadness stared back to her as a perfect reflection of her broken heart; which caused Lilly to quickly look away and return her attention to her bleeding wound.

She started to wrap her wrist with the soft bandage; the blood was seeping through and leaving its blotchy, red pattern with each turn until eventually, it was hidden from view. Lilly turned the faucet on to wash away the blood and return the basin to its pristine white. When satisfied with its cleanliness, Lilly left the bathroom and moved back down the hallway towards the living room.

As she reached the blue, panelled door with its gold-coloured door-knob, Lilly paused for a moment, then opened the door and entered. The little bed with its red racing car bedcover was perfectly made, guarded over by a vibrant yellow Winnie-the-Pooh bear sitting on the pillow.

Lilly sat down on the bed and picked up the book that lay on the bedside table under the lamp; the title *"Pinocchio"* was neatly embossed in silver on the front cover. As she flicked through the pages, Lilly remembered his beautiful laughter when she had read his favourite book to him at bedtime. We never did get to finish it, she thought to herself. She clutched the book to her chest, not wanting to put it down. As she looked around the room she took in the toy box filled to the brim with colourful toys, the wooden bookcase laden with various books neatly stacked and the little brown boots standing together as loyal companions.

It was so very quiet and had been like that for a long time. She could still smell him; still feel him, as if he were an unseen part of her. Lilly finally placed the book back down and with a deep sigh, stood up. She left the room and gently shut the door; locking the memories in a timeless vault yet again.

Lilly walked into the living room and stood for a few moments staring out of the large panoramic window. Her eyes settled on the swing set and slide, lightly covered in snow in the yard, silent and still. Behind it lay the vista of Lake Michigan in all its expanse and beauty. The view reminded Lilly of the glorious sunsets that the lake shared each evening; like a blessed, endless gift, freely given with no thought of return.

Continuing with her reminiscence, she turned her gaze towards the large, jarrah-framed picture hanging above the stone fireplace. Knowing this would be the last time, she savoured every last reflection and memory being offered up in this moment. The photo was her favourite, a moment captured forever in the annals of time. The Point Betsie Lighthouse, with its fire-red roof, surrounded by icy-white snow mounds, stood proudly in the background. Lilly looked at the photo of herself, locked in a loving embrace with her young son and husband; laughter and love etched on their faces. A snowman with stony eyes and stick nose, crowned with a woollen blue and red beanie, completed the montage.

How quickly life can change she thought. It seemed as if grace had turned on her in apparent rage. "Why? Why me?" she had asked the heavens. The answer had never come, despite her desperate prayers. But now it didn't matter. Nothing mattered to her anymore. It was too late for answers, even if there were any. With her reminiscing complete, Lilly decided it was time to leave. She moved slowly to the kitchen and collected her car keys and the rope that lay patiently awaiting its purpose on the kitchen table. She took one final look around, satisfied that everything was in its place, left neat and tidy the way she had always preferred.

Lilly walked slowly towards the front door and took her jacket from the hall stand. As she opened the door the cold air slapped her face and entered her warm lungs. Putting her jacket on, she left and shut the door behind her. She stood for a moment on the porch looking at the surrounds of her peaceful neighbourhood; scattered leafless maple trees patiently awaiting the return of their green leaves in spring.

Lilly walked down the steps to her Volvo parked in the driveway and lightly covered in snow. She brushed away the snow from the windscreen, feeling the iciness bite into her bare fingers. Climbing into the driver's seat, she placed the rope on the passenger seat.

As she slowly reversed her car into Lake Michigan Drive she headed back towards the village of Empire. Lilly had lived in the village since childhood; enjoying the adventures of the national parks and sunny days on the beachfront with her family. Her parents had eventually moved to Florida in search of sunshine and her sister, now happily married with children of her own, followed her husband's new work promotion to Toronto. Despite missing them dearly, Lilly had decided to stay on with intentions to raise her own family here. She hadn't spoken to them in months as her deep despair took its hold and she withdrew into its dark cave of isolation and solitude.

As she passed the Manning Lighthouse, she contemplated the multitude of lighthouses that dotted the shoreline of the vast Lake Michigan. Each lighthouse was a symbol of an enduring legacy and commitment by its keepers to ensure a safe passage home for the lake's adventurous seamen. The guiding light illuminated the darkness and revealed the hidden shores. A loss of a single life was considered intolerable.

She pondered the irony of her own situation. Where was her

lighthouse? What happens when a soul is so bruised, so lost on the sea of darkness that the light of life can't be seen through the storm? Who guides the way then, when the will to live is lost? No-one, she thought, no-one. She had never felt more alone than at that moment in her life. A war raged in her mind and the ache in her heart was relentless. Her hand moved to clutch at her chest, clinging tightly to the front of her jacket. How she wished she could reach in and take hold of her heart in her hands and comfort it, to stop it from its constant throbbing of pain. "Please God stop it, please," she spoke out loud.

She turned her car to drive one last time up Empire's Front Street. It was quiet. In summer the village was filled with tourists enjoying the beach and the nearby Sleeping Bear Dunes, but in winter the village enjoyed a peaceful solitude. Lilly slowly drove past the market and tavern, then the Secret Garden gallery with its quaint ornaments displayed in the window; everything carried with it a host of memories.

As she drove the image of her husband flooded her mind. The month since he had left had felt like eternity, but the scene replayed clearly in her mind as if it had happened only a few moments before.

He had stood there in front of her in the very room she had just left. With intense rage in his eyes and anger in his voice that seemed to erupt from a hidden place that could suppress it no longer.

"He was our son, for fuck's sake Lilly."

"It was your responsibility to keep him safe; was that too hard? Was that *so fucking hard*?"

"Richie trusted you to do that for him. He trusted you."

"The day he died, I died as well. Know that. You lost both of us that day."

"All I know is that I can't forgive you; there's just no place inside me

5

where I can find any forgiveness. There just isn't."

"I can't forgive you. I can't forgive you."

Those had been the last words she heard from her husband's mouth. "I can't forgive you". He had then turned from her; picked up the bag he had packed and walked out the door. He might as well have plunged a knife into her heart in that moment; the result would have been the same. His words had inflicted a mortal wound, destroying what little life she had left in her. Already unable to forgive herself for the death of their son, her heart couldn't endure such a deathly blow and it now propelled her towards an inevitable destiny in search of atonement.

Lilly snapped her attention back to the present, realising she had arrived at her destination. She drove into the car park, relieved there were no other vehicles present, ensuring her the privacy she needed. She turned off the engine and left the keys in the ignition. She gathered the rope off the passenger seat and opened the door; her leather shoes crunching the thin layer of snow underfoot as she stepped out. The white sign declaring Empire Bluff Trail welcomed her. This was a familiar spot, as she had been here many times before to enjoy the trek to the top of the bluff and its spectacular views of the lake. Today though, the surrounding forest of beech maple would serve a different purpose.

As she commenced her slow walk along the trail the silence engulfed her. She began to feel an overwhelming sense of peace, a feeling of being liberated from within. Her awareness expanded at the feeling of being part of all that surrounded her: the trees, the sky, the snow. It was like she had ceased to exist within the boundaries of her own flesh and had become a living part of what she was looking at. For the first time she experienced quietness in her mind, free from the constant barrage of thoughts ebbing and flowing like relentless waves crashing on to the shore.

After a short walk she reached the number two marker and turned to look back at where she had come. Her single shoe prints left in the snow seemed a symbolic gesture of her aloneness. She turned away to her right, making her way into the forest off the trail. Two old, rusted wagon wheels revealed their presence above the snow on the ground next to her. She touched them, knowing that they were a historic reminder of the past when this area was used as a farming district.

With the rope in her hand, she continued to walk. Just a little further from the trail, she thought. As she moved she looked ahead, quietly surveying the trees to find the right one.

As she took the next step onto the soft snow underfoot, the solidity she expected disappeared as the ground gave way beneath her; plunging her down into darkness.

CHAPTER 2

Lilly's rapid descent to the bottom of the pit, like Alice down the rabbit hole, was an undignified arrival of sprawling legs and arms, accompanied by the loud crash of rotten timber boards. She lay there motionless for some minutes, entombed in dirt, snow and broken wood; her breath having been sucked from her body in the sickening thud of her landing.

She lay there for a few moments until she had consumed a replacement of air back into her lungs with deep heavy breaths, her body beginning to shake with the shock. Eventually she dared to move, slowly at first, satisfied she hadn't managed to kill herself prematurely and arrive in a version of hell. Lilly tentatively propped herself up, her aching back finding support in a solid wall behind her. Several shattered pieces of board lying across her legs were pushed to the side as she dusted herself off from the dirt and snow on her clothing and hair.

She looked up towards the light that was reflecting downwards upon her, forming a perfect circle that framed the outline of a grey sky and leafless maple tree branches observing her predicament below. Lilly made a foggy calculation that she must have fallen at least eight metres. The feeling of being trapped enveloped her as she observed the circular stone wall that surrounded her. The realisation that she had fallen into an old well fell into place like a completed jigsaw of disparate pieces finally coming together to reveal itself. Along with this realisation came an explosion of anger and rage bursting to the surface. Her mind became consumed with the thought and feeling that God was yet again demonstrating some persistent conspiracy to turn her life into a living nightmare.

"Damn you! Damn You! Damn you!" Lilly screamed upwards to the heavens, at the same time throwing snow, dirt and pieces of

timber against the walls of her cell. The sounds of her intense sobbing were interspersed with her loud vocal expressions claiming damnation.

"Damn you, damn you, damn you" she repeated, until the words tapered off into silence, where only the sound of her sobbing remained.

As the emotional storm inside her began to subside, Lilly found some composure. She turned her eyes upwards again and affirmed her initial thought that there was no way out of this well except up. The rope that now lay beside her had miraculously transformed its role from one of salvation, to now become a symbol of the futility of her situation. Self-rescue was not an option.

She looked at her wrist in search of her watch to see how much time had passed. Instead she saw the bandage, prompting a memory that her watch was comfortably sitting on the bathroom basin where she had placed it earlier. Her solitary confinement seemed complete with this inclusion of timelessness. There was absolutely nothing she could do but sit and wait. Any previous delusion that she held any power or control over her own destiny was now completely revealed for the illusion that it was; and with that thought in her mind she burst into hysterical laughter. The great cosmic joke had her. Lilly couldn't even remember the last time she had laughed so uncontrollably. Maybe she had finally descended into madness, insanity she thought.

It was in that moment, with endorphins flooding her body that she became aware of something very strange happening. The walls of the well started to become defined by lines of light, as if an artist with a white fluorescent pen was drawing the well on a black surface. Her laughing stopped as this mysterious change in her surroundings absorbed her attention. She shut her eyes, thinking she was hallucinating, willing it to disappear. However, on opening them again, the lines of brilliant light were still there.

An image then started to emerge in front of her, arising from the same incandescent light. It was the shape of a man, sitting with legs crossed and hands clasped in his lap. By now Lilly had become extremely agitated in reaction to the hallucination coming into form before her eyes. Thinking that she may have been more injured than she realised, Lilly began running her fingers around her head and through her hair, feeling for injuries. This can't be real she thought, this can't be real. Her fingers settled on a large lump at the back of her head. As she pressed on it pain shot through her body.

Lilly repeated out loud to herself, "It's not real, it's just a hallucination. I've hit my head, that's all. It's not real."

Her attempt at reassurance was not working particularly well as the image continued to take on more detailed form. She watched, filled with anxiety, but also with an intense fascination at the illusion her brain was performing without her apparent conscious participation.

The image of the man was quite stunning. His short, wavy, brown hair was brushed back, framing a handsome, older face sporting a closely cropped beard. The eyes that stared back at her were the darkest she had ever seen, yet exuding overwhelming warmth. His lips were too beautiful for a man, yet fitted well with such a handsome face. He was clothed in white pants and a white linen shirt, buttoned to the top. An embroidered pattern of gold and purple circles ran down the middle of the shirt, each containing a small black dot in the centre.

The image now seemed complete in its revelation. To Lilly it now looked more like an elaborate, colourful hologram with dimension and depth, rather than its vague beginnings as a black and white mirage. It looked so real. Her curiosity couldn't be contained any longer, and she reached out to touch the image. However, her hand completely passed through the hologram, being completely devoid of solidity.

"I love you very much you know," he said softly to her.

Lilly recoiled in absolute surprise as the holographic image of the man spoke, ramming her back hard into the stone wall behind her and quickly pulling her curious hand back towards her chest. Her eyes widened and she was frozen with fear. Yet again her mind raced with the notion that she was delusional.

He spoke again, slowly and quietly, this time with an accent that was clearly noticeable,
"I love you very much, you know. You don't have to be frightened."

A holographic illusion that speaks with an accent, she thought, feeling considerably crazier than she even did minutes before.

"It has been a long time since you have known how much you are loved, hasn't it, my dear? Indeed, you have endured great suffering," he said with such empathy.

Lilly's heart felt an enormous surge of pain run through it like an arrow striking her squarely in the chest. His words had found their sacred mark, causing tears to well in her eyes, despite her trying not to let them free.

Finally breaking the silence that had followed his comment, Lilly asked, "*Who* are you?"

"Well, that is an interesting question, my love. I have walked this earth as a mortal entity many times and have been known by many names. My last life was one of a Bulgarian prophet, so that is how I appear to you today. I could just as easily have manifested myself to you in the form of a lighthouse, but then we wouldn't have been able to chat as we are, would we?" he replied to her with a slight chuckle in his voice.

"I don't understand why. *Am I crazy?* Am I talking to my own illusion like a crazy person? I don't understand," Lilly spoke with distress rising in her voice and feeling utterly confused.

The prophet replied tenderly, "You are not crazy at all. Did you not pray to the Divine for an answer? You asked why, did you not? No prayer ever goes unanswered you know. The answer may not be heard, or come in a way that you expect, but it is never unanswered."

"You are just an illusion, so you can go now, just go. I'm not going to get drawn into this. I don't need this. Just go, *please!*" Lilly spoke with a certain pleading in her voice.

"Well, to you I am a holographic illusion, but to me you are also an illusion, my love. Isn't that curious? The only difference between you and me is our rate of vibrations," the prophet replied, before falling silent for a moment to let his comments settle in Lilly's mind.

He then continued, "I am here to help you. The cause of all your pain and suffering is simply ignorance, that is all. Nobody has ever told you the truth. Nobody."

Lilly was quick to reply, "What are you talking about, what truth? I don't know what you are talking about."

"You gave up my love. Your journey has been a difficult one indeed. So you decided you wanted to go home early…hmm? Well, I am here to tell you that you still have much to do here as a mortal entity. Many wonderful things are yet to happen in this lifetime for you. So I have come to wake you up, to help you remember who you really are. Together we will lift your veil of ignorance and move you to a new mind of enlightened understanding."

The prophet paused, allowing the silence to embrace them both.

 Lilly stared back into the prophet's eyes that seemed to hold her there, trance-like, for some moments. Her mind was spinning, trying to comprehend what he was saying. He seemed to be waiting patiently for her to say something.

With anger in her voice, Lilly finally spoke again. "My son is dead. My husband has abandoned me. Nothing can change that. So don't sit there like you're some god-damn almighty, spinning me this bullshit story about waking me up. It's my choice if I decide to bail out of this hell. This time I get to make the choice, nobody else. It's my choice. So go and be a prophet in someone else's nightmare, because I don't need you in mine. *Got it* ?"

By the time Lilly had finished speaking the venom in her voice was obvious, but the tears in her eyes at the same time belied the strength she was trying to convey.

The prophet waited again patiently, his compassion for her palatable. He then spoke very quietly in reply. "Your son, Richie, is a beauteous soul. You taught him much about the nature of love, even in the short time he was here in this particular life time. His love has never left you, you know. Even when you thought you were so alone, his light is always within you."

"How do you know Richie's name? How could you know that?" Lilly spat back quickly, demanding a reply.

"There are many things about your reality that are hidden from you, my love, including the aspect you consider as death. You believe that you exist only to the boundaries of your flesh that you know as your body; and the death of that body is considered as the end of life. It is this meaning that causes the human entity to experience this limited understanding with anguish and sorrow, an immense source of suffering indeed. Yet nothing could be further from the truth, my love. The demise of the body is not the end of life at all, it never could be."

"You asked the Divine 'Why?' did you not? A magnificent question if ever there was one, indeed. To contemplate one's own existence and the nature of the life you live is a profound quest for the human entity. You see, my love, the truth is never held from you when it is asked for and you stand in receivership, ready with an open mind. Even your own scriptures proclaimed this promise when these words were inscribed:

Ask, and it shall be given you; seek, and ye shall find; knock, and it shall be opened unto you."

"Then tell me why, prophet. Tell me why my heart aches with so much pain that I can't take it anymore. Tell me why a small child has to die. Tell me why a husband abandons his wife when she needed him the most. Tell me why I lost my best friend. Tell me why my life seems so meaningless if there is no-one to love. Answer me that prophet, tell me *why*, I'm listening," Lilly burst forth in utter frustration.

The prophet replied quickly, "Let me tell you, my love, that all of your life has been lived in the valley of ignorance, unaware that in the mountains, unseen by your limited perspective there dwells great causes and purpose beyond your knowledge and awareness. These causes rumble down from above and leave you only to experience the effects that you call your reality. At the core of your being you have a suspicion of sorts, that maybe there is something greater than the life you know, a greater power that reigns. Is that not who you pray to for your answers? Well, I am here to share with you, my love, what lies in those mountains hidden from your view. It is time for you to know the truth because you have dared to ask the great question."

14

"I am going to take you on a journey my love. I will take you to this loftier vantage point of your reality so that you can perceive from a different perspective. It is only with new knowledge that you can ever understand, so I am going to share many new truths with you. I want to help ease much of the pain and suffering you have endured. You will need great courage to walk this path, my love, as I am going to show you your life from a different perspective; as an observer high on the mountain away from the valley you have been lost in.

So just watch, my love .... just watch."

As Lilly watched, the prophet began to morph from a human form into a screen-like projection onto the wall of the well. She felt like she was watching a movie. Her eyes widened as the screen began to play a scene that had been burned in her memory like a laser beam.

CHAPTER 3

Empire, Michigan
26th December 2011

Mitch Andaman struck an imposing figure as he walked into the kitchen of their home. He was a tall man with a muscular build and broad shoulders; an enduring legacy of his military training. His short, cropped, black hair suited him. A strong voice declared his presence to Lilly, who was busy with her back to him, cooking eggs and bacon on the stove.

"Morning babe, have you seen my cap anywhere?"

Lilly turned to acknowledge her husband's question and arrival. She never tired of seeing him in his US Coast Guard uniform. He always looked impeccable in his starched navy blues adorned with emblems and insignia, perfectly hugging the rugged frame of his body. His trousers, with single, stark crease lines running down the centre of both legs, disappeared into highly polished boots reflecting the world around him. She smiled warmly at him and was instantly drawn closer, to retrieve a loving hug and kiss that he was always quick to offer first thing in the morning. At times they behaved like young lovers on a first date, rather than a married couple of six years.

As she embraced him tenderly, she responded to his question, "The last time I saw your cap it was sitting on your son's head".

As they released from their embrace Mitch turned his attention to their five-year-old son, Richie, sitting on the floor playing a short distance away near the Christmas tree. He seemed totally absorbed with the Transformer toy he had received from Santa the day before. As Mitch moved nearer to him he had to step over empty boxes and

Christmas wrapping paper that still remained after yesterday's festivities.

"Hey Sport, have you seen Daddy's cap? I need to go to work," Mitch asked as he ruffled his son's hair in obvious affection.

Ignoring his dad's question, the young boy replied, "Daddy, can you help me with this, the wheels don't work."

"Mate, help me find my work cap first and then I'll have a look at it for you," Mitch said firmly.

Lilly had always loved the sound of her husband's Australian accent. It just added to his irresistible charm, she thought. As she placed a plateful of breakfast on the table, she watched her two beautiful young men begin a search of the living room for the elusive cap. A smile settled on her face as she did so.

"I found it," yelled Richie in delight, holding in the air a cap bearing the blue and gold seal of the Coast Guard emblem above the peak.

Mitch grabbed his son around the waist and hoisted him off the ground, hugging him like a grizzly bear with a cub, growling noises and all. He placed the cap on his son's head and pulled it down over his eyes, which left the small child giggling with delight.

"OK, bring your toy over here and let me have a look," Mitch said, placing his wriggling son back down on to the carpeted floor.

As Mitch sat down at the kitchen table he hoisted Richie on to his lap. His attempt at eating eggs and bacon while simultaneously contorting the Transformer toy into all sorts of poses was proving to be more of a challenge than he had anticipated.

"It's meant to look like a fire truck daddy, not like that," said his son, who was critically evaluating Mitch's every move.

"Well, this Transformer can look like anything it wants to buddy," Mitch replied, attempting to cover his tracks of failing to conquer the little toy.

After about five minutes, Mitch conceded defeat and decided that going to work was a better option.

Lifting Richie off his lap, Mitch spoke with his mouth half-full of bacon, "I gotta go mate. I'll give it another shot after work."

As Richie returned to his place near the Christmas tree, Mitch placed his cap firmly on his head and loaded his pockets with car keys and mobile phone that were waiting on the bench.

Lilly approached Mitch for another hug, saying, "Have I ever told you how much I love a man in uniform?"

"Well as long as I'm the only one in a uniform that you're loving sweetheart, that's fine by me," Mitch replied as he locked Lilly in his arms with a firm embrace.

As they kissed tenderly, Mitch then reluctantly pulled apart remembering he had to go to work. "I'd love to stay here babe, but I have to go. I'll give you a call if I'm going to be late."

"OK, that's fine. I love you," Lilly replied lovingly.
"Love you too," Mitch replied as he grabbed his jacket and duffle bag and then turned towards his son.

"See you Sport, be a good boy for mummy won't you?"

Looking up for a brief moment from his attention with his set of new toys, Richie yelled back, "Bye Daddy".

As Lilly followed Mitch to the front door and closed it behind him, she felt a surge of love flow through her body. She couldn't believe how lucky she was at times; she wondered what she had done to deserve these two beautiful young men in her life.

Returning to the kitchen, Lilly cleared the breakfast dishes from the table. A bowl of half-eaten Corn Flakes remained as Richie's feeble effort at having breakfast, before being lured back to his new stack of toys.

She looked over towards her son playing quite happily by himself and said, "Well, it looks like it's just you and me today, Richie."

He looked at her for a brief moment and then promptly returned to what he was doing, with an obvious contentment with the situation.

The next couple of hours passed quickly as Lilly busied herself cleaning up the Christmas aftermath left from the day before, washing dishes and doing the laundry. After calling her mother in Florida, Lilly made herself a fresh cup of coffee and finally sat down for a few minutes' rest.

Sitting at the kitchen table, her attention was drawn to Richie sitting by the window looking rather forlorn as he gazed outside. Next to him was the colourful kite sporting an image of SpongeBob that Mitch had personally picked out for him and wrapped as a gift from Santa. Lilly took her coffee and sat down on the carpet next to him.

As she looked out of the large panoramic window facing towards Lake Michigan, she observed a flock of American Robins perched on the snow covered swing set in the yard.

"Are you looking at the birds, sweetie?" she inquired.

With a sad little look on his face, Richie turned to his mother and replied, "I wish I could go outside and fly my kite."

Lilly returned her gaze to the scene outside, observing the snow-covered ground and the clear sky. "Well, you've been stuck inside all week and it's not snowing today. What say we go down to the playground near the beachfront and then we can fly the kite near the lake. How does that sound?"

Richie didn't need to be asked twice. He bounded up with obvious delight and started jumping up and down.

"*Yay!* Let's go, let's go," he squealed, grabbing the kite and running towards the door. Lilly smiled to herself. He was so much like his dad, easily excited, she thought.

"Hang on, hang on, you need your jacket and beanie …. And change your shoes," she yelled after him before he made it to the front door.

Considering their excursion involved only a short trip down Lake Michigan Drive to the playground near the beach, it amazed her how long it always took to get organised with a small child. As they stood near the front door, Richie awaited a final inspection by his mother.

Lilly crouched down to eye level with her son and zipped up his red jacket with its Wiggles emblem displayed proudly over his chest. A cute face of brown eyes and pert nose peered back to her under a blue and white-striped beanie. To Lilly he was a perfect re-creation of Mitch, albeit a smaller version. Placing her hands around his head she pulled him closer to her and planted a wet kiss on his cheek.

"I love you, little man," she said tenderly.

"I love you too, Mummy," he replied in his sweetest little voice before breaking free of her grasp and whipping the front door open to vanish in a flash.

Lilly followed with bag and kite in hand, pushing the remote for the garage door in the process. With Richie safely strapped into the back seat, Lilly reversed the Volvo and began the short journey along Lake Michigan Drive back towards the beachfront. Having arrived in the car park, which had been swept clear of snow, Lilly pulled into a space facing the playground on the shore of South Bar Lake glistening under a cosy blanket of ice.

She noticed only one other car present in the car park. As she hopped out of the warm confines of her car her attention was drawn to a warmly dressed man pushing a little girl on a radiant pink bicycle around the car park. On seeing her alight from the Volvo he waved vigorously and walked towards them.

"Hi Lilly, how was your Christmas?" he asked with a warm smile on his face.

She immediately recognised him as one of Mitch's work colleagues from the US Coast Guard base in Frankfort. "Hello Dan. It was hectic," she laughed in reply. "Looks like Santa left a few goodies at your place as well," she continued, admiring the pink bike the little girl was riding.

"Santa was very generous," he said, looking proudly at his daughter waiting patiently for his return. "What's Mitch up to today, is he rostered on?"

"Yes, he's on day shift. So you have some time off over Christmas Dan?" Lilly asked.

"Yep, I wrangled a few days off to be with the kids. I love Christmas," Dan said, before turning his attention to Richie standing patiently near Lilly with his kite in hand.

"Hi Richie … Hey, that looks pretty cool," referring to the new kite.

The small boy replied proudly, "Yep, mummy and I are going to fly it."

"Well, it's a mighty fine day for kite flying, with that breeze coming in from the north," Dan replied, looking skywards and sounding very professional.

After a brief exchange of further pleasantries, Lilly and Richie left Dan to continue with his cycling lessons and made their way closer to the lake's edge.

For the next 10 minutes, the scene on the lake's shore included a mother and son showing all the signs of multiple failed attempts to get the kite airborne. After untangling knotted string, a lot of running around and a few crash landings, the kite eventually found its peace and started to soar above the frozen lake. The smiling, yellow face of SpongeBob beamed down at them, looking quite superior from its vantage point.

As Lilly stood near her son, who was holding the wad of string, they both looked skyward, enjoying the spectacle of the kite's high-flying antics.

Shouting in absolute delight, Richie said, "Wow! Look how high it is Mummy"

In encouragement Lilly replied, "You're doing an amazing job….how smart are you doing it all by yourself ?"

"I wish Daddy was here to see me. Maybe we can we take a photo to show him?" he continued, looking hopefully up at Lilly for an answer of yes.

"OK, that's a great idea, but I need to get the camera from the car. Are you right for a moment? You're doing really well," Lilly said as she started to walk quickly towards her car.

As she reached the Volvo she opened the passenger side door and delved into her handbag to retrieve the Fuji camera hidden amongst cosmetics, purse and small toys. After finally locating the camera, she turned her attention back towards her son and the lake. It was at that moment when her life seemed to switch to one of extreme slow motion as she processed the scene unfolding before her eyes.

The kite that had been soaring high above the lake suddenly plunged to earth as if an invisible hand had personally switched off the wind on purpose. Then, without a second's hesitation her son started running towards it with his little legs pumping hard across the icy surface.

Lilly screamed the only words she could think of in that blurred second of time,
"*Richie ... Noooooo*".

As the little boy reached his treasured kite he stopped, paused for a brief moment, and then promptly disappeared through the sounds of splintering ice as the lake swallowed him up in one swift bite.

Lilly ran with all the speed she could summon, taking great strides across the frozen lake with eyes firmly fixed on the hole in the ice ahead of her. By the time she reached the gaping wound in the ice she was gasping with breath and overcome with sheer terror that had gripped her heart with its claw-like tentacles.

Ripping off her jacket and dumping her shoes she plunged feet first into the ice cold water. The intense coldness spread through her body and sucked the air from her lungs. The murky water stung her eyes and limited her vision, seeing only a few feet in front of her face. Above her she could see the sheets of ice and a circle of light beaming through the murky water. Flailing her arms around, Lilly desperately felt for anything that felt like her son, panic surging through her trembling body.

As her lungs started to implode through lack of oxygen, Lilly felt her energy start to slowly drain from her exhausted body and her consciousness seep from her. Fighting to hold on for a few seconds longer, her last vestige of awareness was given over to a force drawing her towards the light above her head. As she looked up, a terrified face peered at her through the waterline. Just as she slowly came to recognise the face of Dan, the black veil of unconsciousness descended over her.

The hissing noise of the oxygen mask covering her face lured her out of a deep slumber back into reality, despite her resistance. As Lilly slowly opened her eyes, she struggled for a few seconds to make sense of her surroundings and the outline of several images leaning over her.

"It's OK Lilly, you're OK, just lie still," said a gentle voice, as he lightly stroked her shoulder in reassurance.

As Lilly's hazy focus started to return, a torrent of memory downloaded at a rapid speed into her mind. She instantly shot herself upright from her supine position on the stretcher, casting off the blankets that had cocooned her within her own body heat. The mask covering her face was torn away in the same action.

"Richie ! Richie ! " she yelled, desperately scanning the surrounds for any signs that a miraculous rescue of her son had occurred during her stupor.

With firm hands pushing her back down onto the stretcher, her eyes finally settled on a scene occurring on the frozen lake. Bright yellow barricades marked the area of broken ice with two police officers standing sentry. A final realisation by Lilly, that the other figures present near the open hole on the ice were wearing diving gear, gave way to a blood-curdling cry of anguish that rose from the depths of her soul.

In an attempt to console his distressed patient, the paramedic kneeling beside Lilly spoke in an effort to comfort her. "The police divers will find him Lilly, they'll find him."

Despite the efforts of those around her, Lilly forced her way up to a standing position, pulling a blanket tight around her cold body. She stood there numb and yet trembling at the same time, holding her hands to her face as she wept.

"Please forgive me..... Please forgive me..... I should never have left him.... Please God forgive me .... Bring him back, please just bring him back!... Please God!" Lilly pleaded, bargaining with some unseen force in an attempt to ease her suffering.

Watching with a fierce intensity at the scene on the lake for her prayer to be answered at any second, she noticed the SpongeBob kite on the ice, as if it too was waiting for the miracle return of its treasured owner. Unable to cope any longer with the image of torment before her, she turned herself away from the scene on the lake. As she did so she was confronted with the sombre figures of Mitch and Dan walking towards her in a synchronistic march of despondent comrades.

When Mitch reached Lilly she collapsed into his arms and broke into wretched sobbing. Little did they both know, that as their bodies clung together, united by a common grief, they were thinking the same thought, "Please God, not again."

CHAPTER 4

As the vivid screen confronting Lilly began to fade, the holographic projection of the prophet again returned taking only seconds to complete the transformation. The confines of the well had ensnared her body and prevented her surrender to the overwhelming instinct to run. The scene she had just witnessed had activated a cascade of emotions that had literally transported her back in time, to relive that day in her life all over again. In response, her body began to tremble and shake uncontrollably and her breathing became rapid and shallow. Lilly thought she was going to pass out.

The prophet, sitting opposite her in a cross-legged repose, spoke with all the gentleness that a father would have done so to a beloved daughter. "Just breathe my love, just breathe; this too will pass."

As the wisdom of Lilly's body began to rein back the wild steed of emotions loose within her, she finally managed to speak in a strained voice, "Why did you do that? It was cruel, so cruel."

In a gentle voice the prophet replied, "It would have been far crueller to let you take your own life, my love; to have denied your soul the full experience of its journey and evolution. You are being woken up in the midst of your dream and that takes enormous courage. Cruelty is to leave you asleep, to pretend otherwise and keep your ignorance. This then would have left you to continue to unconsciously create a life of pain and suffering. That is the cruellest act."

Refusing to look at him, Lilly spat back a quick response, "I have no soul; it died that day with my son."

The prophet contemplated her words and then replied lovingly, "It is the soul that manifests the physical body my love, not a body with a soul as you may believe. The body is a beautiful garment, a tapestry of oscillating, vibrating energy so to speak, worn by the soul to sensually experience the great adventure of life in all its duality. To experience a state of forgiveness is to first know its opposite, that of not being forgiven. Your beautiful heart is heavy with the great burden of feeling responsible for your son's death. You have not forgiven yourself, my love."

"There is a great truth that the 'effects' you bear witness to in your reality, come from the great pendulum swing of 'causes', that remain outside your level of awareness and knowledge."

"Who were you to ever control the impulses and spontaneity of a small five-year old child who wanted to run after his beloved kite?"

"What control did you ever possibly have to propel the winds of Mother Nature?"

"How could you ever have known the instability of the ice on a frozen lake?"

"You see, my love, there is nothing you could have done. When a certain event is destined in the journey of the soul, then the synchronicity of circumstances will conspire to bring it to fruition."

"Are you saying that it was my son's destiny to die that day?" Lilly asked, horrified at that thought.

"You are an immortal spirit in a temporary vehicle of mortal flesh and blood, which inevitably perishes. Death is the greatest illusion my love, which eventually reveals the truth that you are an eternal essence, a divine being that can never die or cease to exist. The soul comes to know its eternalness and divine power through experiencing its opposite manifestation, as a human entity with all its limitations and fears."

"It is this fear of death that lies at the heart of all your ego's beliefs and meanings, as it represents the great unknown and has everything to do with loss. There is nothing more fearful for the human entity than a loss of something dear to them, whether it is the loss of a loved one, a loss of love in the form of rejection and abandonment, the loss of status and wealth, even the possessions and objects that the ego identifies itself with. Fear is the greatest motivator of human action and desires."

"Fear is what has brought you to this well, my love. Your fear of a life without your husband and son causes you great uncertainty and distress, a great unknown that is searching for relief and reprieve within the certainty of your own demise."

"So, in answer to your question my dear, yes, it was your son's destiny to play a role in your life's journey, that has brought you to this well and your enlightenment," the prophet replied.

Trying desperately to make sense of what the prophet was saying, Lilly responded, "But he was only five years old. He was so beautiful and loving. It seems such a waste…. such a terrible waste."

"Every person in your life, whether they be a child, lover, a friend or stranger has their purpose and role; even the tyrants and villains that are the bane of your existence. All are present to create a relationship with and to reveal an aspect of yourself that is out of tune with your true divine nature. When the soul incarnates and descends into a particular lifetime as a human form, it becomes amnesic, so to speak, forgetful of its true nature. It knows no-thing of love, humility, forgiveness, charity, compassion and virtues of grace, it knows none of these things. Each relationship provides an opportunity to remember those virtues and attune with the great divine mind and creator. More is learnt in this experience of relationships than could ever be discovered by one-self alone."

"Certain traumas, adversities and cataclysmic events are used to 'speed up' this remembrance. For it is at those times that the mortal becomes open and receptive to change. For evolution is all about change. Your consciousness is participating in evolution, my love, not only your body."

"You taught your son much about love in this lifetime, as you also learned from him. To be able to love beyond any conditions and agreements, to give freely from the heart with no thought of return, is a powerful lesson. Your son's soul journey in the experience of love was fulfilled as a five-year-old; such was the power of not only your own beautiful heart, but also that of your husbands'. Another life incarnation that spans a hundred years may never have experienced the same love that your son did, so the duration of mortal life is not the true measure of a soul's journey, but rather the depth of wisdom gained from the experience."

The prophet paused to let Lilly consider his words.

"I should never have left him alone near the lake. I'm not sure if I can forgive myself, how do I do that? Even Mitch couldn't forgive me, even he can't," Lilly replied quietly, with heaviness in her heart.

The prophet quickly responded, seeking to quell the obvious pain in her question.
"Your husband's attitude towards you is only a projection of his own burden of guilt that he carries within himself. Was he not the one who bought the kite for your son? The human entity has an ingenious strategy of protecting its ego from dissonance, by projecting on to others the emotions it is unable to cope with itself. So you, my love, have accepted his judgement of you without question, as you already carry the same guilt that he has denied."

"The ego that resides within every human physical form is the great arbitrator in your life, forever holding yourself up for judgement, and then dispensing your own judgement or to other entities. My dear, your parents, society's expectations and religions have all taught you that certain behaviours are rewarded and others are punishable. Even if left to yourself, you will continue the same pattern of behaviour, punishing yourself mentally for what you consider as a wrong-doing or sin. You are always seeking redemption because of this great arbitrator forever tormenting you. This is where the seeds of forgiveness spring from, my love, blossoming forth from the concept of right and wrong, good and bad, evil and righteousness."

"The ego of your personality is a creation that is designed to perpetuate the illusion of separateness. This is in direct contrast to the true interconnected and unified reality of the Divine Mind, the source of all creation. Your ego can only ever perceive within a world of relativity, evaluating and judging everything only in relation to something else. Indeed it is a dualistic perspective of existence, and hence everything in your physical reality is continually subject to a judgement or evaluation to give meaning to your ego. What you consider to be black and white, good and bad, or high and low, for example, is only a continuum of perspectives, each one needing the other to be expressed; two sides of the same coin, so to speak, for one cannot exist without the other being present."

"To find forgiveness in your heart, my love is to change your perspective. For you have chosen a meaning for your son's death that brings you great suffering through punishing yourself. Seeded within every circumstance is the opposite. For situations that may be considered adverse, there is always a blessing or something favourable; and for any perceived blessing, there will also be something adverse or challenging. These opposite natures may not be instantly revealed or obvious at the time, but will eventually reveal themselves to you, as that is the paradoxical nature of this reality. Even in your deepest sorrow, my love, know that a blessing will someday come to lift your heart again. For whatever is lost from you is always replaced; trust in that promise."

"So find your peace, my love, and imbue your son's passing with new meaning and perspective. Contemplate what I have told you and find the place in your heart that releases you from feelings of guilt and leaves only the love that is already there waiting to shine. Always know you have a choice; a change in perspective is only a thought away. As you find your own forgiveness, your husband will reflect back to you this change within your heart; for you are both connected emotionally and spiritually. There is nothing you need to do, only to be."

Lilly replied to the prophet with a heavy heart, "If I have such a loving heart, I don't understand why it has to be broken. I feel like I have been smashed upon the rocks of life. Why me? I am a kind, decent person; I have never hurt anybody. It all seems so unfair. There just seems to be no reason, no purpose for living anymore; I've lost everything."

"Man's search for meaning and purpose of existence has endured since the days of antiquity. For seeded in your very existence is this desire to know; a search for the truth, so to speak. It is this ability to reason and contemplate your own existence that sets you apart from the lower planes of consciousness in other life forms."

"No truer words have ever been inscribed than those on the great Oracle of Delphi in Greece, and espoused by Socrates himself:
> *In you is hidden the treasure of treasures.*
> *Know thyself, and you will know the Universe*
> *and the Gods."*

"The quest for self-knowledge is the finest mastery that a human entity can pursue, for it is the search for Divinity itself. The divine nature and essence of man is hidden in the last place that a mortal would ever look, within your self. At times it takes enormous adversities and calamities to provide the catalyst for the mortal to turn away from the ego's desires and venture inwards to find peace and security. The entity often returns as an empty vessel, stripped of the titles, labels and possessions that provided the ego with a sense of identity. Those losses propel the human mortal towards a journey of self-discovery and revelation of their true divine nature."

"Your greatest illusion, my love, is you are not who you think you are.
When you lose the identity of ego labels, such as a mother and wife, or challenge your concepts of self, such as those of being a decent and kind person, then you come to know that you still exist, regardless of whether you are those labels or not. The path to truth is paved in this self-discovery that you are not the ego, but a spiritual essence that is eternal and free."

"Your presence in this well, my love, is a perfect demonstration of this truth. For here you are devoid of time, possessions, labels, or any role such as mother, lover or friend. Every ideal that you have considered as real now exists only within the confines and construct of your own mind."

"You do indeed have a purpose; you are a neophyte of the Great Work, to make known the unknown. Through knowledge you gain the keys of wisdom and understanding that you are the co-creator of your reality. You have now reached a significant point in your soul journey that requires the veil of ignorance to be lifted, to reveal the masquerade, so to speak."

Lilly interrupted the prophet, challenging him angrily, "What do you mean I am the co-creator of my reality? I certainly didn't call upon myself this living nightmare!"

"As you have experienced, my love, the forces of creation lie outside your level of awareness and knowledge, and that state of ignorance persists so long as it is necessary for the soul's development. Many mortals never awaken during a lifetime and continue to create unconsciously a life of hardship and lack, for that is the evolutionary level of their consciousness. There are many different archetypes or themes that a soul can choose from to explore on this physical plane of existence. For you my dear, your Oversoul has chosen an awakening in the midst of life, to clear your distortions of the ego and become a lucid creator with the Divine."

"Much of the new knowledge that I will share with you may challenge your current beliefs and be judged by your ego as sceptical. The ego, by its very nature, is one of doubt and relies on sensually perceiving something to believe its existence. This truth is not one to learn or believe, only to remember; for you will find that at a deeper subconscious level of your being there will be a resonation or intuitive feeling of acceptance."

"Consider this thought; you are living in two realms of reality simultaneously, one visible or perceptible and the other invisible, or beyond your sensory perceptions. As a physical entity in a human body you are only able to perceive your reality through your five senses, operating within your central nervous system. Any vibrational energy and neuronal impulses that are not within the range of your sensory perceptions will not be received at your level of conscious awareness. Your perceived reality, therefore, offers only a small sliver from which to experience physical existence. Even the forms that your eyes fall upon rely on your brain's ability to recognise patterns of light and darkness, to construct an image from memory within the confines of your brain. Turn out the lights and you can't see; a very simple truth indeed. The light waves of photons made visible through the lens of your eyes are, therefore, only those contained within the visible light spectrum; the rest remain invisible to you. The same can be said for the waves of sound striking your ear drums. If the vibratory waves are a frequency beyond the capacity of your neurons to translate as electrical impulses within your brain, then those sounds remain inaudible."

"Your brain, my love, is really the master magician of illusions, creating a world externally to you that appears in three-dimensional perspectives, with shadows of depth, width and height. This sensation of forms and objects being projected external to you is very powerful and sustains the perceived reality of separateness. Even the solidity of matter that surrounds you is illusionary, only created by the arrangement of polarised electrons spinning in orbit around the nucleus of an atom. An atom consists almost entirely of empty space and yet it manifests into the solid forms that you experience through touch, and what gives your body physical formation. So you can see, when I talk about the great divine creator, this is a concept that is beyond the physical, sensual realm of your existence, and can only be alluded to within the limitations of the words I use to describe an invisible deity."

"Do you mean God? Is that what you're talking about?" Lilly interjected with curiosity.

The prophet considered her question for a moment and then replied, "I have purposely not chosen the word God, because it is shrouded in a variety of meanings to every entity; especially the concept that God is an external creator, separate from the physical, mortal being. Instead, I prefer to lead you to a different contemplation that you are the divine creator, experiencing existence through the individuation of its consciousness, manifested into both physical form and formless spirit. When viewed from this alternative perspective, you can then come to understand your physical body as being an instrument or garment, being used by the soul to sensually experience creation. This change in perspective may assist you greatly as it unites you within the womb of creation, rather than disempowering you to believe that you are isolated and separate. From a holistic perspective, you are the Divine, as well as the aspect experiencing the creation; the creator and the created so to speak."

"I like to use the analogy of a little island in a vast sea; on the surface the mass of land appears to be its own boundary of existence, yet beneath the water-line it is one unified whole with the earth's crust. Now, if I stretch your imagination a little further, let's consider the shoreline of this island. Just as you know with certainty that the island does not cease to exist at this shoreline, so too do you not cease to exist at the boundary that is your physical body. Just like the little island arises from an unseen realm beneath the waterline, you and everything you perceive visually or sensually, also arises first from an invisible realm. All creation streams forth from a single, unified fountainhead that is the first cause or breath of the Divine."

"This source has been called many names, such as the Void, All that Is, Infinite Intelligence, Zero Point, Ether, Absolute, Supreme Being or Godhead, just to name a few. I choose to call it the Divine. There is nothing beyond this eternal and infinite source that is omnipotent and omniscience; it is the purest state of being. Everything emanates from this first point of creation. The image of a circle with the point in the middle, such as the ones you may see on the front of my robe, is an ancient symbol that is used to represent this ideal."

"The image of the dot can be considered as the first Word or Logos of creation, that is, the Divine's original intent to experience itself, to bring forth the mandate of 'I exist'. Every aspect of the Divine, whether manifest or not, is in accordance with this original mandate. On your physical plane of existence, this intention embeds itself in every aspect of life, from the smallest atom to the universe itself. All of the universal laws of the cosmos exist to animate and give life to the creations of the divine mind, the great realisation of the "I Am". These laws apply to everything and show no exception or favouritism; they operate regardless of your knowledge or ignorance of them."

"As you may now understand, it is only the ego's own judgement on any circumstance that gives meaning to any aspect of creation as being either favourable or adverse. In truth, every facet of creation carries no inherent meaning, other than the one the ego chooses to perceive through the filter of its own judgements. The divine creator is free to give expression to every possibility of creation as that is its first law, 'I exist'."

"This ignorance of the universal laws is what generates the most fear in the lives of the mortal entity. To not understand the nature of things or know the effects from causes unknown is a phenomenon of an unawakened state of being, a lower level of consciousness, so to speak; as one fears what one does not know. You, my dear, are like a little drop of water in the great ocean of consciousness; you are immersed in the infinite intelligence of the divine mind. I tell you, my love, you are the law giver as well as the receiver of law, as you are a divine being, the Law of One itself. When you come to fully understand and know this truth, you will have dealt your fears a mortal blow; for that which knows has no fear."

"The laws of the universe immerse you within fields of hidden forces that operate continuously to manifest and create what you perceive on your screen of life that you call reality. The law of vibration is one such significant force that is always making its presence felt and experienced; in its simplest terms it means you get back what you put out. Your universe and evolution is all about vibrations; everything is in a constant flux of change, nothing is still. Knowledge of this law is essential to your awakening, for a master can learn to consciously create by vibrations, rather than be buffeted on the sea of ignorance; drawing to your life chaotic events and circumstances."

"To help you best understand this law, is to use a past experience from your own life story to view from the perspective of an observer."

"So once again, my dear, just watch ….. just watch……"

Lilly once again watched, entranced as the prophet morphed before her eyes into a screen- like projection on the wall of the well.

CHAPTER 5

Patong Beach, Phuket, Thailand.
26th December 2004

As Lilly sat comfortably nestled in the wicker chair on the balcony, she gazed at the calm sea reflecting the morning sun and the activity on the beach below. The coloured circles of the beach umbrellas lined up in neat little rows stood like sentries ready to spring into action when their service was required. Tanned bodies of idle tourists already lay relaxed on blue cushioned beach chairs, soaking up the warmth of the sun. The sight of palm trees seemed to complete Lilly's reverie that she was in the midst of paradise.

The sound of the sliding door being opened next to her broke through the daydream and drew her attention instead to her friend, Sophia, now standing there beside her.

"I'm ready; sorry I took so long. My head is still spinning from those cocktails at the Christmas party last night," Sophia said jovially as she was magnetically drawn to the balcony view that her friend was absorbed in.

"Do you realise, Lill, that we would be up to our ears in snow at home? God this is so nice!" Sophia continued with obvious delight and enthusiasm.

Lilly replied with a hint of irony in her voice, "I think we could have been a little closer to the beach though, it's such a long way to walk."

As Sophia edged slightly over the balcony, eagerly looking for any bronzed males on the beach awaiting her reverence, she replied, "Very funny, any closer and we would have the sea lapping at our doorstep. It's a great hotel you chose. At least we can eye off the talent on the beach from here."

"You're such a perv, Soph. Shall we go and relax by the pool and get a coffee?" Lilly suggested, moving herself from the comfortable confines of her chair.

With eager anticipation and already making the move back inside, her friend answered,
"Absolutely, I would kill for a cappuccino."

As the two college friends moved back into their modest hotel room, the two beds lay dishevelled, strewn with towels and clothing; used Coke cans and chip packets added to the clutter patiently awaiting the arrival of housekeeping. Lilly picked up her Hermes shoulder bag, loaded with the day's tourist essentials and headed for the door. As Sophia followed closely behind her, Lilly locked the door and placed the key in the side pocket of her bag.

The two American beauties, with sunglasses perched on their heads, wearing bottom hugging shorts and tight sleeveless T-shirts, ambled their way down the tiled hallway towards the stairs. After the quick descent of two floors, they emerged into the foyer and breezed past the two smiling faces of the Thai women working behind the reception desk, who both greeted them with a warm good morning.

After the brief exchange of pleasantries, the girls made their way outside and chose two poolside, padded recliners with a clear view to the beach. Once nestled in they sat for a moment observing the activity of guests and staff around them. The approach of a waiter dressed in a beige uniform, bearing the emblem of Patong Bay Garden Resort and carrying a small pad and pen, provided a welcome interlude to their musings.

With a beaming smile that seemed commonplace amongst the beautiful Thai staff, the waiter asked them with his best attempt at

English, "Good morning ladies, is there anything I can get you?"

"Good morning. Yes, I'll have a latte with two slices of fruit toast, thanks.
What about you, Soph?" Lilly asked turning to her friend seated next to her.

As Sophia returned the warm smile of the waiter, she replied, "I'd like a cappuccino and the same with the fruit toast, thanks."

The waiter promptly wrote down their order and departed with a purposeful walk back towards the glass entrance doors of the hotel.

After quietly eyeing off the gorgeous waiter as he walked off, Sophia finally turned to her friend and said, "I'm really looking forward to the boat trip to Phi Phi Island tomorrow I had a friend who went there last year and he raved about it. It should be very exciting."

"Well, let's enjoy it while we can, it's back to college for us next week," replied Lilly.

"Do you know where you want to teach once you've finished your degree?" Sophia asked with curiosity.

Lilly pondered for a moment and then said, "Maybe a school in Travesty. I would like to stay somewhere near Empire. What about you?"

"I'm heading for the West Coast, somewhere like Los Angeles. I'm so over the snow in Michigan; I want some sunshine and gorgeous tanned men in my life. But you would have to come and visit me, Lill, I need a best friend in my life," Sophia replied with a slight laugh in her voice.

Before Lilly had a chance to respond her head was propelled

sideways by a large brown football smacking with force into her, causing her Ray-Ban sunglasses to fly off her face onto the paving. Immediately she turned around, looking for the culprit in which to vent her annoyance. Her intense glare settled on a shirtless, tanned young boy wearing red and white boardies running towards her from the direction of the beach.

"I'm really sorry. Sorry about that, sorry! My dad kicked it a bit too hard," pleaded the young boy, whose sandy-brown sun-bleached hair and blue eyes completed his claims of innocence.

As he bent down to collect his football that had landed at the pool's edge, he also claimed the dislodged sunglasses and carefully handed them back to Lilly, in an attempt to restore some lost honour.

"Well just be careful, there are other people around here to consider as well you know," Lilly replied bluntly as he walked away back towards the beach where he had come from.

As Sophia watched the boy walk away, she asked her friend with curiosity, "What accent was that? Australian do you think?"

"I think so. Australians should be banned from resorts, especially football-kicking ones," Lilly replied, her laughter giving away any sentiment of meaning what she said.

Sophia continued to gaze towards the beach for some minutes until she eventually spoke with curiosity at the scene she had been watching, "What's everyone looking at over there? All those people are looking at something going on."

Lilly turned to look towards the beach and saw a large group gathering, staring out to sea. She then said, "I'm not sure, shall we be nosy and go and have a look?"

As she spoke, several guests and some staff, also aroused by the same curiosity walked past them and headed towards the beach. Compelled by the instinct to follow the herd, the girls gathered their bags and walked the short distance to the beachfront.

As they arrived, the view that confronted them was one of a massive area of open beach, devoid of sea water, with exposed rocks and fish flapping around. It was as if the tide had gone out and forgotten to stop at its usual place. Some children were squealing in absolute delight, trying to pick up the flapping fish stranded on the wet sand. The scene fascinated the girls.

"Is this normal, do you think? I don't remember it looking like this since we've been here," Sophia asked Lilly who was standing next to her.

"This is really weird," Lilly replied, her mind racing and confused, instinctively feeling that something wasn't quite right.

As Lilly's eyes were drawn to the horizon she was fixated on an image of a white line that stretched across the entirety of the ocean view. Trying to make sense of what she was seeing, her mind settled on a thought that it looked very much like a breaking wave. As this idea began to settle, a dawning finally broke through into a final realisation and understanding of what she was looking at.

In a petrified voice, Lilly yelled at her friend, *"Oh my God, it's a tsunami Soph... it's a tsunami....we need to get off the beach."*

Grabbing her friend's arm, Lilly pulled Sophia back towards the hotel, running as fast as they possibly could. They were quickly joined by the throng of other people on the beach who had also realised the gravity of the situation looming down on them; the congestion of the fleeing crowd slowed down their retreat.

Lilly and Sophia had only reached the hotel pool when the immense wave of sea water crashed into their backs, knocking them off their feet and into the powerful, swirling rush of water. They were totally surrounded by a whirlpool of brown, murky seawater, carrying with it umbrellas, beach chairs, torn cushions and people, all being swept along violently.

As the force of the rampaging water smashed open the hotel's glass entrance doors, the girls were sucked into the foyer that was now adding the chairs, huge ornamental vases and a statue of Buddha, to its wrath of destruction. The sheer magnitude of the water swallowed them up and forced their bodies beneath the surface; tumbling them around like rag dolls in a washing machine.

When Lilly eventually emerged from her submersion and gulped in treasured breaths of air, she felt her flesh being ripped at and pummelled by the debris slamming into her body. As she was swept unmercifully along she smashed into the wooden staircase, wedging her against the brace structure, knocking the air once more out of her lungs. Holding on to the banister with what little strength she had left, the wreckage crashed into her back as if attempting to dislodge her from her mooring. The sounds of smashing glass and screaming added to the roar of the water around her. She felt like she was in the midst of a raging river that was spilling through the insides of the foyer and out the other side through the smashed doors and windows. Lilly held on with all the determination that knew her life depended on it.

For a time that seemed like eternity, the pull of the water began to subside and Lilly was able to stand, with the water reaching to her chest. Her bag, weighed down heavily with the water inside it, pulled like a weight across the back of her shoulders. Lilly was exhausted and sucked in deep breaths of air, free from water that her lungs were screaming out for. She felt her body shaking uncontrollably from the shock and trauma of her experience. As she felt the trickle of blood running down the side of her face, she looked at the multiple cuts and red welts covering her arms. As her mind took in the extent of her injuries, an assurance that at least she was still alive provided some respite.

This brief interlude was suddenly replaced with the stark realisation that Sophia was missing. Desperately looking around the chaos in search of her friend, Lilly screamed loudly, *"Soph ! Soph ! Sophia !"*

She heard a call come back quickly in response, *"Lilly! Lilly! Over here, I'm over here."*

Lilly turned towards where she heard her name being called and saw her friend clinging to one of the large, round support columns in the centre of the foyer.

"Oh thank God!.....Thank God!...... I thought I had lost you Soph... thank God," Lilly responded, in a relieved voice.

Sophia called back again, *"Help me Lilly, I can't move."*

Lilly's attempt to move towards her friend became a slow and difficult task, as the water was filled with debris cutting into her body and feet. When she finally reached Sophia, she could feel the water around her slowly pick up momentum; starting a retreat of flow back towards the sea from which it had spewed forth.

"Oh no, the water's flowing back. Grab my hand Soph... grab my hand," yelled Lilly urgently, as she reached her friend and extended out her hand, which Sophia gripped firmly.

As Lilly pulled Sophia through the water back towards the staircase, Sophia screamed out in agony, *"Ahhha! .. My foot...my foot... I can't stand Lilly, I can't stand."*

Lilly stopped and wrapped her arm around Sophia's back, trying to help her move through the water, which was pushing against them. With every movement they made Sophia cried out in distress from the pain shooting up her leg.

"Come on Soph, you can do it....We need to get to the stairs....you're nearly there," Lilly urged her friend.

Breathing hard and using all her strength against the force of the water, they finally made it to the staircase just as the full power of the water intensified; this time roaring past back towards the ocean. Lilly lifted her friend up on to the stairs, just enough to be clear of the water. They both sat there breathing hard and shaking from the shock pumping through their bodies. The sound of car horns, small explosions and screaming outside added to the roar of the rushing water inside the foyer and the visual calamity they were both witnessing.

While sitting on the step, Lilly's eyes were drawn to a cascade of blood flowing down the steps in front of her, returning and mingling with water at the base. She then realised the flowing blood was coming from a deep, gaping wound at the back of Sophia's right heel.

Alarmed, Lilly said to her friend, "Soph, your heel is bleeding really badly. I think you've cut your Achilles."

Sophia, who was rocking herself back and forth from the pain, looked down and responded with distress, *"Fuck, it hurts like hell ..... How am I going to get out of here?"*

"We need to stop the bleeding Soph, it's really deep," Lilly said, trying to think quickly about what she could use to stem the flow of blood.

As an idea suddenly fired into her mind, Lilly instantly leapt to her feet in readiness to move and said, "I'm going to grab some sheets from our room for a bandage, Soph. Wait here, I'll be back, just wait here."

As Lilly raced up the stairs two steps at a time, her body felt the searing pain and dull aches from the battering she had endured for what seemed like eternity. On reaching room 207, she pulled the soggy bag from her shoulders and retrieved the keys from the side pocket. Her numb fingers and trembling hands from the rush of adrenalin made opening the door a challenge. Eventually she succeeded and slammed the door open in an extreme state of urgency. On entering the room she proceeded to attack the bed and pulled the white sheets off in one almighty tug, sending the pillows and towels flying.

Standing there for the briefest of seconds she tried to think of anything else that might be useful. For reasons that didn't seem to register in her awareness, Lilly moved towards the sliding door on to the balcony. She stood there with the crumpled sheets held firmly against her chest, viewing a totally transformed scene that had earlier been her vista of paradise. The palm trees had gone, as was the pool, which was now hidden under a murky, brown blanket of seawater. The entire area was a giant soup of rubbish and debris. It was in that very moment that Lilly became a witness to the second massive wave that crashed itself on to the shoreline and exploded its contents yet again into the already shattered remains of the hotel's court.

"Oh God, no!" were the only words Lilly could manage, as she turned and sprinted back out of the room towards the staircase.

With panting breath she clambered down the stairs as fast as her legs would allow. Lilly then stopped in her tracks as she approached the ground floor. The steps below were covered in a torrent of raging water twice the level that it was previously. Her friend was nowhere to be seen.

Dropping the sheets, Lilly stood screaming with panic into the chaotic scene confronting her, *"Soph! ...Soph! ...Sophia!"*

Walking as close to the water as she dared, Lilly looked frantically around for any sign of her friend, again screaming, *"Sophia! ..... Sophia!"*

Standing on the steps, Lilly was finally overcome with the realisation that her friend was gone. As she sat down, hugging her legs, an intense sobbing racked her body; her face contorted into one of absolute despair. With a whimpering voice she spoke out loud to her absent friend, *"I'm sorry Soph ... I shouldn't have left you ...I'm so sorry...I'm so sorry."*

Lilly continued to sit there, in utter shock, unable to physically move. She didn't know what to do any more. She felt numb.

Through the noise of the rushing water and the sound of her own sobbing, Lilly's awareness was slowly drawn to a voice calling out from the wreckage before her, *"Help me, please help me, please!"*

As Lilly looked up, she scanned the devastation before her in search of the source of the cry for help. Her eyes finally locked on to a figure trapped in a compressed heap of debris congested against the wall of the hotel. Only a head and tangled arms locked around the heap was visible as the water rushed past. She stood up, her mind wrenched from one of grief and pity into a sharp focus of how to help the person calling. Her thoughts raced with an inner turmoil of whether to wait for the water to subside, or somehow get the person back to the safety of the staircase. With a realisation that the rushing water would eventually change direction and suck itself back towards the sea, taking the stranded person with it, Lilly knew she had to do something.

"Just hold on, I'm coming to get you. Just hold on!" Lilly screamed out to the figure, at the same time not yet knowing how she was going to get there.

As she stood for a few moments, taking in everything around her, Lilly's eyes eventually settled on the white sheets sitting in a crumpled heap on the steps. A plan revealed itself. Taking hold of the ends of the sheets, she knotted them firmly together. She tied one end securely to the staircase closest to the waterline and outer wall. Using the sheets as a rope, she tentatively stepped into the rushing water, with one hand tightly wrapped around the knotted end of the sheet. The force of the water pushed her against the wall.

Her aching body again felt the exertion of every move, making it painful and laborious, as she fought against the will of the sea to claim her. Every breath became a struggle as the water kept washing against her face and into her mouth; she fought to keep her head above the water. Edging her way slowly along the wall, Lilly came to within a meter of the clump of debris and the figure it held within its clutches.

"Can you reach my hand? Grab hold of my hand," Lilly cried out, stretching her free hand out towards the person, the other still wound tightly around the end of the sheet.

As the figure started to dislodge itself from the pieces of debris, slowly moving towards her, Lilly gradually recognised the form of a boy.

"Take my hand. You can do it. Grab hold of my hand," Lilly yelled in encouragement to get the boy to move closer towards her.

With hands outstretched towards each other, the boy finally grabbed hold of Lilly's hand with all the force that knew his life depended on it. She drew him closer through the water until he took hold of the sheet. With her hand pushed against his back, she guided him along the wall. As he disappeared under the rushing water she would pull him back to the surface, helping him stay above the foaming, brown seawater.

"Keep going! Keep going! We're nearly there!" Lilly shouted, urging the tired boy on.

Little by little the staircase came closer, like an island, beckoning them on to embrace its safe shore. With one final shove, Lilly pushed the boy onto the staircase and out of the water. Following closely behind him, she heaved herself out and then pulled him by the arm further up to the safety of the landing. They collapsed, exhausted next to each other, sucking the air back into their tired lungs.

Waiting until she had recovered sufficiently, Lilly lifted her exhausted body into a sitting position to check on the shaking figure lying next to her. The sight of the red and white board shorts and wet, sandy-brown hair brought with it an immediate recollection of the boy with the football. His back was covered with cuts and bruises already emerging as angry, red blotches on his tanned skin.

Lilly gently rubbed his back in comfort and said, "You're OK now, you're OK, you're safe. What's your name?"

As the young boy slowly sat up, still shaking, he looked at the scene before him as if affirming for sure the reassurance by his rescuer that he was safe. He replied, "Zac, my name's Zac. I can't find my dad; I don't know where he is."

With these words the realisation that he had lost his dad came to settle and he started to cry. Lilly placed her arms around his shoulders and pulled him in a little closer. With gentleness in her voice she reassured him. "It's OK Zac, we'll find him; if you survived I'm sure he has too. We'll find him."

As Lilly looked at the chaos before her, she prayed for the truth to her words; may they find both her friend and the boy's dad.

After pausing for a minute, Lilly continued, "My name's Lilly. How old are you Zac?"

"I'm twelve years old," Zac replied quietly.

"Is there anyone else you came with? What about your mum?" Lilly inquired again.

"No, it's just me and Dad; my Mum's not alive. I live with Dad in Perth. This was meant to be a Christmas present. How am I going to find my dad?" Zac said, as he again started to cry.

"We're safe for now, Zac. I'm sure when the water level drops there will be people to come and help. So we just need to sit tight. Are you hurt anywhere?" Lilly asked with concern.

Looking more comfortable with the thought that there would be help arriving soon to look for his dad, Zac wiped the tears from his eyes and answered, "I'm just sore, I think I'm OK."

"I've got a room upstairs, so I'm going to take you there so you can lie down. I'll go up onto the roof to see if we can get some help, OK? Shall we do that?" Lilly asked as she stood up and held out her hand to Zac.

As Lilly helped Zac to his feet, she gently put her arms around his shoulders and they made their way up the stairs.

She looked behind one last time in a lingering glance at the desolation behind her and silently prayed for Sophia.

CHAPTER 6

As the image before her started to fade, the holographic projection of the prophet again returned in front of her. Lilly felt like she was being taken on a rollercoaster ride of emotions that was turning her stomach inside out; she wanted to get off.

In a viscous tantrum of anger she started to throw pieces of broken wood that lay around her at the prophet as the words spat from her mouth, "*Damn you! Damn you! Damn you!* So Sophia had to die as well? Is that what you're going to say? Does everyone I love have to die? What about all those thousands of poor people that lost their lives that day; was that destiny as well? *Was it? Was it?* What type of so-called Divine causes so much suffering? Answer me that. *Go on answer me that!*"

As the pieces of wood passed through the hologram of the prophet and clattered off the wall of the well behind him, he sat there composed and silent until he eventually replied,
"It is only your ego, my love, that judges and condemns, as you know not why things occur, nor to what ends or purpose are met through those events. All suffering arises from this ignorance, as it is a sign that you are still yet to remember your perfect state of divinity. There is nothing that moves the human entity faster into this remembrance and understanding of their true divine nature than those of a catastrophe or disaster."

"Consider what the entity often refers to as the human spirit: that unseen essence that seems to arise to the surface in times of trial and tragedy. The separation of one individual from another, whether by colour of skin, culture, nationality, age or creed, melt into insignificance in such moments, leaving only a common unity of humanity. Such events provide an opportunity to demonstrate the latent or hidden attributes of the Spirit, where courage is revealed through fear, compassion through cruelty, altruism through greed or love through hate. Your own circumstances, my love, have revealed this truth already on three occasions, where you demonstrated enormous courage to preserve the life of another; even one that was a stranger to you. Adversity can bring an entity face-to-face with their worst fears, in order to conquer and overcome; to make you fearless. A Master knows that more is learned about your true nature in the storms of a high sea than is ever learned in the calmness of still waters."

"The spiritual journey is designed to bring you to a realisation that your fears are a manifestation of your ego. As long as you continue to believe that your life exists sensually only in flesh and blood, as your ego will have you believe, then your actions and motives will always be governed by the fear of death; whether you are conscious of this or not. When disasters and death are only perceived from this limited view or perspective of your ego, then inevitably you will experience enormous suffering and grief. The great paradox of life is that it is this very suffering that provides the catalyst for the entity to walk the spiritual path in search of peace and love within, having not found it in their external reality."

"Such experiences have been called 'the dark night of the soul', as great losses usually accompany this period in an entity's life. However, just as you are experiencing my love, Providence then moves to assist the mortal being into a spiritual awakening or enlightenment, bringing forth new knowledge and understanding to the entity's search for truth."

"Every person in your life is a connection of souls on a journey together, each playing a role in the development of the other. So may you be comforted by this knowledge, my love, that those you consider as lost to you in human form, remain forever connected to you spiritually. As you may come to gradually understand, the nature of events in your life are indeed hidden beyond your conscious awareness, but are never devoid of divine meaning and purpose."

As Lilly listened to the prophet's gentle words following her outburst, a feeling of peace settled over her. Once again the silence allowed her to consider what he had said, until after a moment she ventured with another question, "Why would souls want to experience such suffering for their development, why do they do that?"

"For the greatest prize of life, my love, wisdom.
Now, this is where new knowledge becomes essential for your expanded understanding, as your perceptions are limited by your memory and your current knowledge. Just like the walls of this well are clearly defined around you, so is your reality defined and expressed through only what is known to you. This is what I have meant when referring to you as being a neophyte of the great work, making known the unknown. To change your reality is to change your perception."

"When I talk of wisdom, you are limited by the context of a human entity's understanding of this word. When I speak of wisdom I come from an expanded perspective and therefore speak of it with all my knowledge and understanding as being one of vibrations. Wisdom is a vibration. As I have said to you previously my love, everything in the Universe is vibrational, subjugated to the great law of vibration."

"There is a wonderful axiom to this truth taken from the ancient Hermetic philosophies that may assist your understanding that says: 'As above, so below; so below as above.'
What these words affirm is that whatever scale you contemplate in the universe, whether it be the microcosm or the macrocosm, the same laws apply, only differing in degrees of manifestation."

"If I were to take you to the loftiest vantage point of life, you would see all of creation emanate first from the Divine Mind, the fountainhead of creation that I attempted to describe earlier to you. The Divine Mind is absolute; nothing is beyond it as it is eternal and infinite. The rate of vibration for the Divine is so incredibly fast that it appears to be at a complete state of rest, free from movement and omnipresent, pervading all space. It is consciousness in its purest state of love, whole, complete, powerful and all-knowing."

"Now, remember also my teachings earlier that all of creation is in accordance with the mandate of 'I exist', for the Divine to experience itself as the creator and the created. So as well as being the source of creation, the Divine is also the medium or ether through which energy is transmitted by means of vibration. Then further still is the phenomenon of life in all its aspects, whether visible in form or invisible spirit, which exist as expressions of these vibrations. This triune of creation is what the ancient civilisations often reflected in the structure of pyramids: an enduring symbol of man's reach for the heavens."

"So when understood in this context, whether it be a human form, a soul or even the term wisdom takes on a very different meaning when understood as expressions of vibrational energy. A soul is a higher vibrational rate than a human form, and when expressing the soul's development in seeking wisdom, this then comes to mean evolving or ascending to a higher rate of vibration."

"Are you understanding this concept my love, is it making sense to you?" the prophet asked.

"I'm doing my best, this is all new to me, but I'm trying to. So are you saying that I am a vibrational energy and so are souls?" Lilly replied.

"I know this may be difficult to understand at first, especially as much of what I am describing to you is unable to be visibly seen as your ego prefers. But I will continue."

"Yes, the soul is a vibratory aspect of life, just as your physical body is, only differing in the rate or speed of vibration. Let me put this in a context of evolution, which may be more familiar to you. Before evolution can be understood there must first be an involution. By this I mean that because the Divine is absolute there can be nothing outside it, nothing vibrates or exists beyond it. So for the Divine to experience itself as creation, the vibrations must be slowed down in speed. As the vibrations are stepped down, the consciousness becomes individuated into units of expression: such as the oversoul, then onto the higher soul or self, then to the astral bodies surrounding you, then to the soul and finally into physical form. This is called involution or a descent into matter. Whatever is perceivable to you as gross matter or solid form is the end result of this involution."

"Evolution is the reverse process, where the vibrations of entities are raised in vibration or stepped back up in ascension. This is what is often referred to as Jacob's ladder or stairway to heaven. The solidity of gross matter loses its solidity as the vibrations increase in frequency, and the invisible entities move higher to new realms or planes of existence that match their higher vibration. This is the evolution of consciousness, always cycling through transformations of endings and beginnings, in a divine journey to experience all levels and aspects of creation; then a return to the wholeness, perfection and unity that is the Divine."

"Now it is important for you to remember that even though the vibrations are expressed at different frequencies or rates of speed, they are emanating from and through the same source, being the Divine Mind. Nothing is actually separate from the other, but contained within each other, a nested hierarchy of vibrating energies that are all interconnected; the saying, 'All is One and One is all', best describes this concept."

"Creation is like a giant spider web spinning from the divine mind and returning to this source eternally; a constant, ever-changing flow of energy in a circle of life. Once you understand this, you will see that as I have claimed, there is no death, only life eternal. Those loved ones that are lost to you are only lost in visible manifestation, their love and essence can never be separated from you, as everything is forever connected within the infinite Divine. There is only transformation, as one life form ends there is always a new beginning, a new adventure. To ever consider yourself as separated and isolated from those you love is only a perspective of your ego in its limited understanding of the true nature of reality. So find some peace in this understanding my love; you are the ocean of energy as well as the wave that arises from it, as well as the current that flows and the experience that dwells. To know yourself as a multidimensional being, existing on different vibratory levels or planes of existence simultaneously is a powerful insight."

Before the prophet could continue, Lilly interjected with curiosity, "You said before that adversities make us fearless. If I am a human entity as you describe me, then fear seems to be a natural part of living. Why then are humans made to experience such fear? Why not let our experience of life be only loving and joyful?"

"A wonderful question my love, your contemplation of this learning is leading you towards questions that you would have never considered before."

"Now, to answer your question let us remember the axiom I mentioned earlier, 'As above…so below,' and also the understanding that all laws exist on all scales varying only in degree. So if the divine mind, being the 'As above', is seeking to 'Know thyself' within the mandate of 'I exist', it individuates into aspects that are opposite manifestations of its true divine nature; being one of a whole, loving, perfect, powerful and all-knowing deity. To put it simply, the Divine comes to know itself through experiencing the opposite of itself. If you then consider yourself as a human entity existing 'as below', then you are also experiencing yourself as an aspect of the Divine in a manifestation opposite to your true nature as a divine being; just as the Divine is, but differing only in degree. This is the role of your ego, to create an aspect of yourself that feels separate, unloved, fearful and forgetful of its true nature. Like the Divine, you come to 'Know thyself' by experiencing the opposite of your true divine nature. The ego becomes like a distortion, a vibration that is out of tune with the orchestra of the divine mind. Your spiritual journey or enlightenment is the process of attuning your vibrations back in to harmony with the Divine."

"Your ego is a fearful being because that is the survival nature of the programming within your brain's anatomy. Remember that matter, like your body form, is a lowered vibration that has coagulated into solidity. Fear is a very low vibration. Your body is not some accident of nature, evolving from the survival of the fittest mentality as your Master Darwin would have you believe. It is a sublime design of spiritual proportions created purposefully for your soul's journey and development. Now, here is an understanding that will stretch your boundaries of belief. The garment that your soul wears, being your physical body, has been purposely designed to attract and create into your physical reality, the experience of the very thing you fear. This is the law of vibration at work."

"You are a powerful co-creator with the Divine my dear, whether you are aware of it or not. Your body emits a powerful broadcast of vibrational frequencies into the ether that you are immersed in. This vibration then attracts its equivalent form; a like to like, so to speak. In simple terms, you reap what you sew If your predominant emotional state is continually fearful, being anxious or afraid, fearing a loss or lack of something, then this becomes your point of attraction. All your powerful emotional states of being will reflect back to you in your physical reality as circumstances and experiences that match. Why, you may ask? So that all of the attributes or vibrational states of being that are out of tune with your true divine nature are made obvious to you, so you know where a change in vibration is required. It is a feedback mechanism, a tool for learning."

"When I said to you that adversity makes you fearless, then it rides upon the reasoning that fears when confronted and overcome will vanish. When you come to an enlightened understanding that you create your own demons through attracting them to yourself for realisation and release, then you reclaim the divine power within you. So previously, when I spoke of the human spirit being revealed through trial and tragedy, it is the Divine moving you from the lower vibrations of fear, cruelty, greed or hate to the higher spectrum of vibrations more attuned with the divine mind, being one of courage, love, compassion and altruism."

"Fear is a great motivator for change, which is why it is used in spiritual development. If the soul existed in a garment that only ever knew continual joy and bliss then the human entity would never move from such a place of comfort. It is indeed only the pointy rock irritating the entity's posterior that forces it to move, not the supple one. A desire to know a truth must first be rallied in the human entity before a truth is made known; otherwise it falls upon deaf ears and a closed mind."

The prophet waited for his words to settle in Lilly's mind. She looked away from him for a moment, letting herself digest the information he was sharing. After a few minutes she turned her eyes again towards him and spoke with a heavy heart, "I'm having difficulty accepting this idea that I create my worst fears. I feel like things have happened *to* me, rather than anything I've done to deserve it. I need some help with that one."

"There is nothing in this knowledge I share with you, my love, that has anything to do with deserving anything that happens to you; that is an ego judgement only. Let me for a moment lead you to a point where you can view your present life as an unfoldment, where everything that has been destined in your journey has its perfect time and its foreseen place. If you were to view your life from this perspective you would see that there is always a cycle and rhythm, where there is an ebbing and flowing of some events favourable and some adverse. Just as an entity would learn little from a life of eternal joy and bliss, so too would the other extreme of too much adversity crush the entity into hopelessness. The pendulum swings with equal measure of compensation, always seeking equilibrium in your unfoldment. This creates the conditions most favourable for your soul's development."

"This unfoldment of your life could be likened to a book, a scroll, or a manuscript so to speak, and the title is called 'The Book of Life'. This is not the only time that you have ever lived, so each chapter contains the wisdom gained from each of your soul's experiences into physical form. Your lifetime may be as brief as one page or as long as fifty. Each chapter endeavours to evolve your consciousness, to wake you up in your dream and become lucid within the divine mind of the creator. Every event and circumstance in the unfoldment of your life is designed for the soul to come to realise the duality of all its virtues and integrate them into the wholeness of the Divine."

"If you examine this book closely, whether it is yours or another's, you would find the common theme of love and all of the dramas the loss of love evokes. Fear reveals where the opposite virtue of divine love is not felt; it is the vibrational opposite."

"Look closely at your own life my love and you will see this truth. It is easy for a human mortal to love another when that love is returned on the conditions and agreements that arise from the needs of the ego.
But how do you love a son when he is no longer physically present to return that love you have given?

How do you love a husband who has abandoned you?

How do you love a friend who has walked away, washed you from their life?

How do you love with a broken heart … hmm?

That becomes the challenge, doesn't it? It is very easy to bring a human entity to the brink of destruction; you take away that which it loves."

"Do you remember the first words I spoke to you? Do you remember?" the prophet asked Lilly.

Lilly quickly replied, "I love you very much."

The prophet nodded in agreement and then continued, "Yes, that is indeed so.

Do you remember how your body felt when I spoke those words to you?

That is because at the deepest level of your being those words resonate with the divine love that is your essence. When you feel loved you are in harmony with the divine mind; there is no fear, because it is your natural state of being. Your heart is the most powerful broadcaster of vibrations of love. It is your ego's fear that distorts this powerful vibrational broadcast into a lower coherence, out of tune with the Divine. So you end up attracting the loss of something you love, rather than creating from the power of the bestowal of love without fear."

"Now, let's delve a little deeper into this teaching on fear as it is this distortion of vibration that is the source of your deepest suffering and torment; it is your greatest limitation as a mortal entity. Yet a change of perspective is all it takes to remove fear from your reality and all that it attracts."

"Imagine your ego as a shadow of your true divine nature; it is created as an opposite manifestation and polarity to that of the

Divine. You are born with a genetic programming and cultural upbringing that is founded in lack, or a negative polarity. Your ego is seeded with desires and needs that are always seeking fulfilment. Now, because the ego is a shadow of your divine nature it sees everything as separate and external to yourself, so the satisfaction of those desires and needs are always sought from sources external to you. Your ego does not know love as a divine essence, but rather as a feeling that something is missing, a yearning for completion so to speak. So you go in search of fulfilment from those people and circumstances external to you; rather than realising that love is always coming from your own internal power first."

"The only love that a human entity knows is that which comes with certain conditions and common agreements: a sense of ownership. Such is this drive to feel loved that an entity often morphs their own behaviour and will to the needs of the other, because it becomes fearful of its loss; to become unloved. When those agreements and conditions of the needs of the ego are withdrawn or no longer met, then the relationship breaks down and you experience the pain of rejection. So you can see, my love, that fear of loss lies behind the motivations of many of your relationships.

This limited perspective of what the ego considers as love, creates a very cold species indeed. There have been more unmerciful and ghastly deeds done in the name of ego love than you can imagine.

The great truth is that the majority of your fears have been learned as a child from your parents, teachers, peers, religions and social consciousness; they don't actually belong to you."

"Do you remember the words of your mother that you thought of earlier today?" the prophet asked Lilly.

She thought for a moment and then said, "I think it was, 'the hardest thing about life is living it, the rest is easy'. Something like that."

"Indeed so. Little do you realise that as a child you store away these beliefs given to you and your life then follows a certain self-fulfilling prophecy. Those beliefs then drive your ego as a personality with a habitual way of thinking and responding to the world around you. Your beliefs drive your predominant attitudes and your attitudes drive your state of being. It is those persistent states of being that are your vibrational frequency being transmitted into the ether and returning to you. As I have said, my love, the Divine is always responding to who you are being. To be able to respond differently to your circumstances, to break free of habitual responses and reactions of your ego is the challenge. Nothing can change the hall of mirrors that is your physical reality reflecting back to you until you change your inner mind: that of your beliefs, attitudes and fears. Fear is a choice; change your mind to change your reality."

"Let me share with you a little story to help you understand what I speak of;

In a little village in the hills neighbouring the forest,
there was a mangy dog, a more neglected specimen
you never did see. Its fur was full with lice and fleas
that bit at the creature's skin unmercifully. This mangy dog
was never tethered and roamed freely in the village but never
to the forest. A small boy, who daily threw little morsels of
scraps to the mangy dog to eat, was the only one who acknowledged
its pitiful existence.

One day when the mangy dog was lying in the sun on the edge
of the village near the forest it was met by a wolf who had
ventured out to investigate the dog nearby. The mangy dog
who had only ever heard about wolves, but had never encountered
one before, bowed down in submission, fearful and shaking.

"Why do you bow to me dog?" the wolf asked with curiosity.

"Because I am fearful of you," replied the dog.

"Why are you fearful? We have not met before and I have not harmed you," the wolf asked.

"Because that is what I have been told; not to venture into the forest because wolves are dangerous and will eat me," the dog replied.

"Well you have been told an error," the wolf said. "I am a free beast who is enslaved by no one. I fend for myself and eat heartily of what the forest provides for me in aburdance. I do not need you or desire you mangy dog. So, I ask of you, why have you chosen not to be free also?"

The mangy dog considered this unusua question and then replied.

"Because I am loved and I am loyal to those who love me. This is all I know."

"Then let me show you true freedom, mangy aog. Your loyalty is an illusion. You wear no collar but you are tethered by your illusion to those who neglect you. This is not love. You are just as powerful as me, mangy dog, you are no different. Come, let me show you."

"But I am frightened," the mangy dog said shcking.

"You only fear because it is unknown to you. Once you know, you will have no fear. Trust me."

So the mangy dog and the wolf left together and vanished into the forest, never to be seen again.

After a few days, the scraps of food thct the small boy had left started to gather, remaining uneaten. The boy wondered at the loss of his mangy dog and thought to himself in his sadness, "But I loved you."

"You see my love, everything in the universe is to do with consciousness and energy, as that is what creates the physical reality

65

that you perceive. The divine mind is self-aware just as your own mind is; it is pure consciousness. It is the mind that creates matter. Whatever you focus upon and give energy to creates the matter of your physical experience. Your beliefs and fears are a powerful creative force."

"Once again your Scriptures confirm this truth, when it was inscribed; *'As a man thinketh in his heart, so is he'*."

"Everything brought into a manifested reality to be made known and experienced begins with a thought. The first Word of the Divine that brought forth the birth of creation was a thought, 'I exist'. Remember that all vibrations emanate from the Divine; so thoughts are powerful vibrations that are seeking their manifestation and expression into life. They are seeking their likeness. Thoughts become like two lost lovers in the mist of the quagmire of life searching for the other. Time and space do not limit or impede them; they will find each other if that is their bequeathed destiny."

"To help you in this understanding , I will show to you an image that is not known to you personally. It is a memory of your husband's that I will share with you. In time and space he may have been separate and unknown to you, but your destinies were on an inevitable path of union.

So once again, my love, just watch........."

CHAPTER 7

Bagram Air Base,
Parwin Province, Afghanistan
0300hrs 26th December 2004

The sound of snow crunching under the fast, heavy pounding of running combat boots broke through the silence of the crisp early-morning darkness. As the shadowy figure reached the door of the B-hut located on the fringes of the US-held air base, he burst through the door and snapped on the lights, promptly lighting up the room in a flash of fluorescent brilliance.

The sergeant moved swiftly through the room, clapping his hands and thundering in a loud voice to awaken his sleeping team, *"Move your asses boys. Move! Move! Move! We're on. It's game time. Briefing room in 5 minutes."*

The eight bodies that only seconds before had been laying peacefully in a comatose dream state on their bunks, were now rallied and brought to life in a frenzy of activity.

As the muscular body of Mitch Andaman unfolded from the cocoon of his sleeping bag, he paused on the edge of his bunk and rubbed his eyes. His focus settled on the body opposite him, who was already up and dressing rapidly in the combat fatigues and boots that were being pulled and laced at a speed not decent for that time of morning.

Having completed the task of securing his boots, the figure of US Marine Corporal, Richard Steiner, turned his attention to his colleague sitting opposite him and said, "Fuck, you look like shit, you Aussie prick."

Mitch was just as quick to respond with the same tone of affection afforded him by his mate, "Well, at least I'm not a Yankee princess like you asshole, fuck you."

The two soldiers continued their usual banter of insults which had become commonplace since their first meeting at Camp Marmal in Germany, seven months prior. Task Force 373 had been set up as a covert squad, tasked with the job of eliminating chiefs and warlords of the Taliban and Al-Qaeda. Mitch found himself as the only Australian, seconded from his usual role with the SAS regiment because of his sniper training and expertise. The group of eight had become tight, isolated from the other coalition forces due to the secrecy their roles commanded.

Having now dressed in combat fatigues, adorned with armoured chest plate and Kevlar combat helmet, Mitch stood with the group in the briefing room facing their commander, Captain Dwayne Harrington. In front of him on a small table was a model improvising rocks, dirt and cigarette packets, in an attempt to map out the target area where they were shortly headed.
Mitch looked upon his leader with enormous respect knowing him as a West Point grad and a seasoned campaigner in the original invasion of Iraq; Afghanistan was now in his field of fire.

"Good morning gentlemen," the captain started with a firm voice. "We've received confirmation a brief time ago, that the intel being received about a possible meeting of Al-Qaeda operative Atman Zawahiri with a province warlord is confirmed.
Zawahiri is our Jack of Clubs gentlemen, a priority target, so we don't want to fuck this one up. In forty minutes we will be transported by two choppers to a drop zone approximately five kilometres from the target area, being the village of Alia Bad in the Korengal Valley."

As the words Korengal Valley were released from the mouth of their commander, Richard and Mitch turned and looked at each other;

with Mitch muttering quietly to his friend, *"Fuck! I hate that place."*

The grimace on Richard's face concurred with his colleague's explicit judgement of their impending destination.

As their commander proceeded with his team's briefing using the model in front of them, he finally neared the end, paused for a moment then said, "As you all know, we've been planning this one for the last month. Today's our chance to nail this son of a bitch. Our advantage is the weather and an early morning strike. At least the snow keeps the rats in their cave."

The captain then turned his attention to Mitch.

"We want a clean shot on this one today, Mitch. We get in, take him out and then we're out of there before they know what's fucking hit them. The last thing we want is to get nailed down in a shit storm with the Taliban. It's your show, Mitch. If you can get a clear shot then confirm and take it. If you can't, then we have orders to blast the compound with the AT-4, leaving nothing standing. There are civilians in these compounds, so collateral damage is not my preferred option."

Mitch nodded, while imagining what an AT-4 weapon, designed specifically to destroy tanks and fortifications, would do to anybody standing in the way. He replied confidently to his captain, "Roger that Sir, I can do this."

Satisfied with his reply, the captain turned to his team and bellowed, "All right, let's get kitted up and be on the tarmac in fifteen minutes. Let's roll."

As Mitch started to move he turned to Richard and said, "Of all the fucking shit holes in the world, Zawahiri chose the Korengal Valley for his tea party, fuck me."

"It's all paradise bro', it's all paradise," Richard replied, laughing at his friend's response.

Having kitted up, Mitch stood with his team members on the tarmac. Strapped to his webbing on the back was the M-16 Infantry assault rifle and over his shoulder his prized tool of trade, the M-24 sniper weapon. As the two fighter helicopters landed on the tarmac they threw up the loose snow and a blistering wind causing Mitch to put his gloved hands up to shield his face. The loud, thundering noise of the rotating helicopter blades shattered the peace and quiet of the early morning. As they watched, the side doors of the helicopters were slid aside accompanied by the sergeant yelling above the din of the swirling blades to board.

Mitch jogged the short distance across the tarmac and climbed aboard the war ship. He strapped himself into the seat and then inserted the earpiece of his radio firmly into place. Having tuned the radio dial to the designated satellite frequency, Mitch then tested his communications with Richard sitting next to him.

"Hawkeye to Playboy are you receiving me? Over."

"Copy that, Playboy receiving you loud and clear, fuckwit," Richard replied with a laugh in his voice.

With that response, Mitch turned and looked at his friend, then promptly gave him the 'bird' with his middle finger raised and then laughed.

As they sat there in silence during the forty-minute flight, Mitch looked at the faces of his team members as they stared intently forwards, their game faces on. With their drop zone finally looming towards them through the mountain darkness, the voice of their commander crackled through Mitch's earpiece, "Five minutes to drop, prepare to exit."

With this command the team all stood and started to connect the rappel ropes attached to the deck of the helicopter. As the doors were slid open on either side, the ice-cold wind sucked itself inside the cabin and their warm lungs. Mitch lowered his night vision goggles attached to his helmet and everything took on a green and white glow. He then manoeuvred his body into position onto the landing rail on the outside of the helicopter, with the rappel ropes held firmly in his gloved hands. As the pilot held the chopper in a hover twenty yards above the ground, Mitch jumped clear of the railing and descended rapidly to arrive on the snowy ground in a firm jolt that rattled his body. He then watched as the rope he had just disconnected from returned at a rapid rate to the belly of the helicopter.

As he stood for a few moments on the snowy mountainside he saw his other team-mates starting to gather together. His commander's voice again crackled into his ear, "OK let's hook up and get moving; we need to be in position before sunrise."

The two scouts took point and started heading up the mountain with the team falling into place behind them in single file. Mitch held the M-16 assault rifle to his chest and followed the green and white form of the soldier in front of him up the steep incline towards the top. The extra weight of the sniper rifle secured around his shoulders added to the load he was carrying through the rocky, snow-covered terrain. His breathing was heavy and formed a misty cloud with each deep breath he exhaled. With his muscles aching he reached the top and began the descent down the other side with a few glimmering lights of the Alia Bad village ahead confirming they were on target.

When the group finally came to a halt they had the advantage of still being on the higher ground, looking down towards the L-shaped compound that was at the outer edge of the village. With the captain's orders being delivered through his earpiece, the group spread out to take up position. Mitch knew he had a range of 800 yards to work with; such was the power of the sniper weapon and scope at his disposal. As he brushed away the snow from the rocky ledge he had chosen, he set the weapon up on the bipod stand and then manoeuvred his body into a shooting position. He pulled the lever bolt of his weapon back towards himself and heard the familiar sound of a round entering the chamber as he released it.

As he lay there, the sky gradually took on a red haze as the sun began to peak over the snow- covered mountains to the west. Removing his night vision goggles, Mitch looked at his watch; as he did so, his solitude was disturbed by the appearance of Richard who cleared a spot next to him.

"Hey bro', the boss wants a clean ID before you shoot, so I'm your spotter," Richard said, with a cheeky grin on his face and pulling out his binoculars.

"Fucking brilliant, I've got the guy that needs glasses to take a piss each morning," Mitch responded with his crass humour.

As they sat propped against the rocks, Mitch looked through the scope at the compound that was meant to be housing the Al-Qaeda chief, until he settled on a battered white combie van parked near a doorway.

Looking through binoculars at the same time, Richard commented, "Do you see the combie van? He must be still in there."

Mitch replied, "Yep," as he lifted his head from the view of the scope and looked skyward and then at his watch again.

"Sunrise is right on time," Mitch stated before returning his eye to the scope.

As they sat there, both locked in an intense focus of their target area awaiting any movement, Richard broke the silence and turned to face his colleague saying, "Mitch do you remember what I told you to do if I get hit?"

"You're not going to get hit, mate. We've got another two weeks of this shithole and it's finished with. We're going home. So you're not going home in a body bag," Mitch replied without moving and maintaining his eye on the scope.

"I know that, but do you remember what I told you to do with the letter? Just so I know; that's all," Richard persisted.

Still not moving a muscle, Mitch replied, "Yes, I remember mate."

"It's inside my helmet, I brought it with me, OK?" Richard replied, taking off his helmet and pulling out a crumpled envelope tucked inside it.

Mitch turned to look at his friend and saw the letter being held in his gloved hand. He replied, "Fuck, have you got a death wish or what? Put it away and get your helmet back on before some bastard blows your head off."

As Mitch watched his friend place the envelope back inside his helmet and then strap it firmly in place, he sighed and then said, "I take the letter to your parents state side."

"I'm all they've got. I just don't want some asshole in uniform who doesn't give a fuck tossing it on their doorstep. I just need to know that all bases are covered bro'," Richard replied, satisfied with his answer from Mitch.

Mitch returned his focus back towards the compound and pressed the butt of the rifle firmly into his shoulder and cheek. As they lay there, the sound of the captain's voice came through his earpiece, "How's it looking Hawkeye? Over."

"All good Alpha ... In position ... good eyes ... minimal wind ....
Over." Mitch replied.

No sooner had the words been sent when the sight of activity in the compound below sent a burst of adrenalin rushing into Mitch's heart and body.

"Here we go.... show time," he quietly said to his friend, who held the binoculars firmly to his eyes.

Four men had emerged from a door-way of a stony hut all dressed in familiar Afghan pyjama-like robes and headdress; long stringy beards dangly from their faces. One held a small child nursed in his arms, as they stood for a moment talking near the combie. As Mitch scanned each face, looking for his target, he settled on one; the Jack of Clubs, whose head was now locked onto the white target of his scope.

"Confirmation of target, the one with the kid," Richard said firmly, without looking away from his binoculars.

"*Fuck!*" Mitch replied; his mind racing with the unexpected twist that had doubled the degree of difficulty in taking out a moving target at 600 hundred yards without killing a small child in the process. His heart was pounding so fast he could feel it in his chest, beating a rapid rhythm against his rib cage. He attempted to slow his breathing down, just as his training had instilled in him; his bare forefinger softly pressing against the trigger, awaiting its short journey of release. His mind was at war, take the shot or not; he had seconds to make a decision.

"Target confirmed. Send it!" Richard prompted him.

Mitch felt like he was frozen in time; his finger refusing the will to move. The breath in his body had ceased all together. His only vision was one of intense focus through the eye of the scope that kept swapping from the target's head to the child's head and back again.

"Target confirmed. Send it !" Richard repeated again, with urgency in his voice and now turning to look at Mitch.

As Mitch's finger finally started to slowly press against the trigger the scene in front of him exploded into a massive fireball of red flames and black smoke, accompanied by a deafening noise. The force of the blast reached him at a rapid rate and pushed against his face and body. He lifted his head from the scope and butt to take in a scene of black smoke rising up and rubble and dust snowing down on the compound that he had been observing. There was nobody left. Mitch sat in stunned shock at the total obliteration of life that he had just witnessed.

"That went well," Richard commented in an obvious tone of sarcasm as he too took in the scene of devastation before them.

Before Mitch could say anything, the sound of the captain's voice burst into his earpiece, "Sorry Hawkeye couldn't wait. Move in. Move in. Base wants a positive PID."

"Fuck! They want a positive identification. There's nothing left of the motherfucker; what's to ID?" Richard stated in frustration as he began to get up and move.

Mitch quickly rose, hoisted his sniper weapon around his shoulders and armed himself with the M-16 assault rifle lying next to him. Together they moved down the mountain towards the compound, joining up with the captain and other team members as they got

75

closer. With his weapon up at face level ready to fire, Mitch was on full alert and aware they were entering the enemies' home ground. As they arrived at the open area of the compound, he stood looking at the burning shell of the combie and the remains of bloodied body parts lying all around him in the rubble; he felt like throwing up.

With two men perched in a squat position near the walls of the stone hut providing security, the rest of the team started scouring the remains looking for anything resembling some body part to identify. Mitch started kicking at the bloodied rubble and car parts with his boots, not wanting to touch anything that looked like flesh. Just as his boot flicked over a twisted combie fender, a spray of dirt at his feet signified an incoming volley of bullets that peppered the ground and walls around him.

"Take cover, take cover, incoming enemy fire," the captain standing nearby screamed at his troops, who all started to run into the open doorway nearby.

As the group huddled at the open windows of the hut they sent back a volley of rounds towards an unseen enemy.

"Where the fuck is that coming from? Has anyone got eyes on where the firing is coming from? " the captain yelled, as he attempted to get a position on the enemy fire through the open window.

As Mitch crouched near the open doorway, with his assault rifle pressed firmly against his cheek, he scoured the area with an intense focus that the adrenalin pumping through his veins afforded him. His eyes settled on a motionless uniformed body, lying face down on the ground about fifteen yards away in the middle of the open compound.

"Soldier down. Soldier down. We've got a casualty Sir, " Mitch screamed towards his captain, on the realisation that the body was

one of their own.

"Do we know who it is?" the captain sent back.

As Mitch scanned the stony insides of the hut from his position near the door, he mentally noted which of his team-mates were present; a sudden coldness ran through his body as he slowly come to realise who the casualty was. He replied, "It's Steiner, Sir."

Mitch felt his stomach churn yet again. As he watched out through the door his mind was racing until it finally settled on an idea that he knew in his heart was crazy. He yelled to his captain and team members, who were still firing off random rounds towards the open terrain to the north of the compound, *"Give me covering fire, I'm going out get him!"*

As his eyes locked with the Captain's for a brief second, in a silent exchange that needed no words, the Captain bellowed, *"Let's lay down some covering fire. Let's do it! Fire!"*

His orders were immediately followed by a rapid burst of small weapons fire from inside the hut towards the open field.

Mitch bolted out the door, keeping as low as he possibly could to the ground, firing off his own weapon at the same time. As he did so, puffs of dirt spat around him from bullets being fired towards him. Quickly making it to the figure lying on the ground, he grabbed the back of the webbing and dragged him at full pace straight ahead into a gaping bomb hole in the stone wall of the hut opposite.

Breathing hard, Mitch placed his gun down and gently turned over the limp body of his friend. Two glazed eyes looked up at him from a bloodied and dirtied face.

"I'm bleeding out bro', I'm bleeding out," Richard whispered, barely able to speak.

With all the blood on his battle vest and cams, Mitch tried to work out where the blood was coming from, at the same time trying to reassure his friend, *"It's OK mate, just a small gash that's all..... stay with me buddy..... stay with me.....don't close your eyes."*

Mitch's hands finally found a gaping wound in the neck and shoulder area that was pouring blood. With that discovery, he quickly pulled a pressure pad from the small medic kit on his webbing; he pressed it hard against the wound, endeavouring to stop the bleeding.

Looking into his friend's dimming eyes, Mitch said frantically, *"Come on mate, stay with me. You get to go home..... I still owe you a beer remember? Come on! ..... come on!...... don't you bail on me!"*

As Mitch watched, his friend's eyes lost their light and went dark. His struggled breaths stopped.

"Fuck! Fuck! Fuck!" was all Mitch could manage to say as he felt the anger rage up inside his body. He stood up and paced back and forth with his hands on his helmet, the anger stirring in his guts; he felt like he was being eaten up from the inside out.

"Fuck! mate... I'm sorry...... I'm sorry.... I should have taken the shot.... Fuck! Fuck! Fuck! I'm sorry .... I'm sorry."

As Mitch paced back and forwards he picked up loose rubble on the floor and threw it at the walls of the hut, trying to ease his distress.

The voice of his captain being received in his earpiece came through clearly,
"How's it going in there, Hawkeye?"

Mitch took in a couple of deep breaths in an attempt to compose himself and then responded with a cracked voice, "Fatal wound, Sir. We'll need a medivac. Over."

"*Shit!* ….. Sit tight. We've got a bunch of Apaches coming in to soften up the area before we get picked up. Should be fifteen minutes at the latest. Hold your position. Out."

"Copy that. Out," Mitch responded.

As Mitch stood there, he looked around the shambles of the hut. The room was a mess, with the opposite wall also a gaping hole. He bent down and picked up a piece of patterned rug, shaking it loose of dirt; he then placed it over the body of his friend. He picked up his assault rifle and sat quietly, leaning against the outer wall near the blast hole, lost in his thoughts of guilt and despair. He realised that the shooting had stopped, it was eerily quiet.

It was in that moment of silence that he heard the sound of whimpering. He realised it was coming from inside the hut. He stood, lifting his rifle to his cheek in readiness to fire and moved slowly towards the hole in the stone wall opposite him. Leaning against the wall he peeked slowly around, with his weapon leading the way.

His wide eyes settled on a small girl squatting in the corner; black, matted hair laced with dust and dirt. Her grimy, bloodied face and teary brown eyes locked on to his with a look of absolute terror. Around her lay the four dead bodies of a man and woman as well as two small children.

Mitch lowered his rifle and spoke softly to the little girl as he moved closer, "It's OK sweetheart. It's OK, I'm not going to hurt you."

As Mitch squatted down near her, she began to shake even more.

"It's OK, it's OK, you're safe," he said in a gentle voice, trying to reassure her again.

Mitch then noticed that the girl's lower left arm below the elbow was a chunky mess of bone and flesh, barely held together.

"Let me help you, you're hurt. Let me help you, OK?" Mitch spoke as he pointed towards her injury.

As he put down his rifle, he retrieved a pressure pad and bandage from his medic kit secured to his webbing. He showed them to her and pointed at her arm, seeking her understanding that he was going to bandage her arm.

"I'm going to wrap your arm, OK? I'm going to cover it up OK?"

Mitch started to put the padding on her arm and then the bandage, speaking softly as he did so, "What's your name? I'm Mitch. My name is Mitch. Do you understand? What's your name?"

The little girl, still shaking and looking firmly at Mitch through wide, brown, teary eyes, finally managed a reply with a quietly spoken voice, "Zahera."

"Zahera, yes? Is that your name? Zahera?" Mitch asked, nodding his head.
"How old are you? You look about ten years old, is that right, Zahera?"

The little girl was silent, not seeming to understand what he was asking. As Mitch finished bandaging her wound, he gently lifted her off the ground. "Let's get you out of this room."

He carried her back into the room where the covered body of his mate lay still on the floor and placed her against a wall. As he did so, the voice of his captain came through his earpiece again, "Incoming friendlies, Hawkeye, keep cover and brace yourself. Over."

Mitch quickly responded, "Copy that. Over."

He again raised his weapon and took up position near the hole in the wall, watching as three Apache helicopters flew overhead, unleashing machine-gun fire onto the open terrain where the enemy had been located. Mitch watched as the area became lost in a haze of dust and smoke as a relentless rain of firepower unleashed itself on the insurgents below. He watched patiently as the Apaches continued to strafe the area, grateful for the air support and impending rescue. Eventually, two rescue helicopters landed on the open ground, spitting up a cloud of dust around it.

"We're out of here Hawkeye. Let's go. Let's go," came the command of his captain through his earpiece.

Mitch replied, *"Copy that. I'm coming out."*

As he jumped to his feet, he moved towards the lifeless body of his mate and hoisted him off the ground and across the back of his shoulders. Mitch exited through the hole in the wall and dashed with his load towards the open doors of the helicopter. Two crew standing near the open doors assisted Mitch in laying the body of his comrade onto the deck of the shaking helicopter.

Trying to make himself heard through the thundering noise of the helicopter blades, Mitch yelled, *"I've got one more to come. One more, just wait."* Then he turned and ran back to the compound.

Mitch ran back into the hut from where he had come, approached the girl and picked her up. "Come on Zahera, let's get you out of here."

Running back towards the helicopter with his second treasured load, his team-mates watched from buckled seats inside, patiently waiting for him before they could take off. The little girl was taken from his arms by a crew member as he was hoisted on-board into the cab; the sliding doors were slammed behind him. As Mitch sat on the deck he breathed in gasps of air and felt overwhelming relief as he felt the helicopter taking off.

He looked over at the girl who was now wrapped in a blanket and being tended to by a medic. Next to him on the deck was the body of Richard on a stretcher covered by a blanket. He sat there for a few moments with his hand on the lifeless body, until he eventually pulled the blanket back to reveal the face of his friend. Mitch undid the strap of the helmet and gently removed it from his friend's head. He took the envelope that was inside, looked at the scribbled, handwritten address on it and then placed it securely in the pocket of his fatigues. Covering the body again with the blanket, Mitch pulled his exhausted body up off the deck and into the seat, buckling himself in. As he looked out the window next to him and watched the Korengal Valley rush past below, he thought to himself, "Such is life, mate."

CHAPTER 8

Lilly watched as the scene once again faded from view and the hologram of the prophet returned in its place. Allowing the image to settle in her mind, the prophet remained silent, until eventually Lilly spoke with some heaviness in her heart at what she had seen.

"I knew about Mitch's friend, Richard, who died in Afghanistan, but he never spoke much about the war. Our son was named after him, you know."

"Yes indeed, my love, I know.
Now let me ask of you this question to consider. Have you ever contemplated where does an act of courage arise from ..... hmm? I say to you, surely not from the ego that is entrained with its instinct to survive, to maintain its body and flesh. No, surely not.
As you have experienced, courage is not found at the level of ego reasoning; for if it was there would be no acts of heroism, none what so ever. Courage rises beyond the ego, beyond fear, as it is an act straight from your essence of divinity, from your heart; it is an act of love."

"I have said to you, my dear, that fear belongs to the illusions of the ego. When confronted and conquered there is a natural emergence of your divine essence, founded upon the powerful energy of love. When you act with courage in your heart, you are in alignment with the will of the Divine itself, you are at one; there is no fear. It is like the sun that patiently waits behind a cloud; you never have to seek it out, go looking for it, for it reveals itself when the cloud moves aside. Being divine, my love, is really not so hard as it may appear, it's what a mortal entity fights so hard not to be."

"Maybe the act of war is the greatest of love stories, regardless of what side it is perceived from. A soldier's love for his or her country, for comrades and freedom; the surrender of one's own life so another may live, is an act of enormous courage and love indeed. You may believe that it is the circumstances of your life that you find yourself confronted with, be it a war, disaster or the dramas of life, that create who you are; indeed I say to you, my love, rather it reveals *who* you are to yourself. From the moment of your birth and through every step of your earthly pilgrimage you attract that combination of conditions and circumstances that reflect your own strengths and weaknesses, your virtues and judgements, your own purity and impurity. The great enigma of 'Who am I ?' will never remain a mystery to you; as your reality is designed to reflect back to you the answer to this question at every turn of events in your life. Whether you choose to love or loathe yourself, either way the tapestry of your soul's bodily garment is sewn in this revelation. You see, my love, your life is not so much about *what* happens to you, for those cards are dealt upon you; but rather about what you *do* with the hand you have been given to play." The prophet paused for a moment to let his words again settle in Lilly's mind.

Lilly replied solemnly, "Why have you shown me these images from the past? They distress me and remind me that I can't change anything. I can't change the past and correct my failures that cause me such pain. What is the point of dragging things up to confront me?"

The prophet responded quickly to her question, "You are lost, my love, in a stormy sea of regret and remorse. By contemplating the taking of your own life, it is a powerful sign that you have plummeted to the depths of hopelessness; you can see no end to your depression and despair. The ego is an entity of certainty and control, and the thought of ending your life provides the macabre comfort that you have regained some of the lost power over your own demise. Hopelessness is a dangerous place to dwell, as it prevents you from learning from your experiences and continuing on with your journey."

"Never seek to change the past, no matter how distressing it is. For hidden within every event of your life is great purpose and meaning that propels you forever towards greater wisdom and understanding that may never have been made known to you without its eventuation. One of the greatest blessings of insight that arises from a place of despair is the natural emergence of order from the chaos of mental turmoil. Your breakdown takes you to the limits of the ego's genetic programming and boundaries; you reach your wit's end, so to speak. Just as surely as the walls of this well confine and imprison you, so too do the limitations of the ego's habits and automated responses enslave you like the mangy dog in the story I told you before."

"All of the emotions of distress, whether they be sadness, anger, guilt or shame, reveal to you where change is required. Remember evolution is all about change. The Divine is a creative energy always seeking to evolve consciousness to higher levels of complexity. Creativity naturally emerges from systems that are transitioning from chaos to order; it is a natural part of the evolutionary process. Self-creation is the highest expression of this process. You are the alchemist, my love, a creature of the Divine, transforming the lead weight of your ego, into the gold that is your divinity."

"A spiritual enlightenment is designed to turn you inwards, as change to your external reality begins with the change to your mind first. Your Master Gandhi had great understanding of this ideal when he said, 'We must be the change we want to see in the world.' To not understand how the organism that is your physical body functions is your greatest limitation. How do you change something if you are not aware of the nature of your own existence? Your ego will never consent to the great unknown that change represents until it is pushed to the limits of functioning, until it breaks. Only then does it become open to change to end its distress and suffering."

Lilly interjected and said, "How do I change then? You said I have a genetic programming. I am who I am and I can't change that, just like my circumstances that have happened to me."

"Consider this then, my love, in answer to your question. Think of the caterpillar that dreams the dream of becoming a beautiful butterfly. Does it not forego its comforts and stop behaving like a caterpillar? It stops eating, makes a bed for itself and goes to sleep dreaming of a day it can soar like a butterfly. Seeded within its genetic identity it has the capacity to do this; to turn its fat, little body to gel, to sacrifice its entire caterpillar being and become the fire of change. Then one day it emerges, born anew, transformed into a creature of beauty and freedom, never again limited by the confines of a sluggish, crawling body that was one of the caterpillar. Now if the Divine can seed within the DNA of a caterpillar the power of self-creation and transformation, what makes you think for one second that you are created any differently? That you too, do not have seeded within you the ability to dream the dream of a better day. Is that not where hopelessness and despair bring you to the brink of? To move and drive you to the point of re-creation, to dream the dream, to imagine a lofty thought and ideal that maybe you can start again when everything has been lost from you."

"Just like the caterpillar, your soul clothes itself in a chemical garment. When I said to you previously you are writing the Book of Life; then you must come to understand that no chapter should be redundant of the one prior to it, just as it must also be so that each chapter sets the stage for the one that follows it. With this in mind, know that your parents are chosen to provide you with the chemical garment that will provide the emotional texture of your life experience; you in effect become your mother's fears and your father's tears. Your ego, which is your temperament and personality, is predestined to carry the DNA passed to you genetically, that allows you to have the behaviour required to meet your soul's journey of development. This DNA is then expressed, or switched on, by the nurture of your upbringing and the nature of your social environment. So yes, my love, you do have a genetic programme that you have been purposely given, to create the attributes of your ego which become the shadow of your true divine nature."

"Now, do you think that the Divine would ever create such a beauteous creature like yourself and not give you a path to salvation, or not give you the ability to liberate yourself from mortal limitations and suffering, or ever remember your state of all-knowingness like that of the Divine itself? Of course not, that is what enlightenment is all about; a revelation and path to the knowledge that leads you towards liberation from the manacles of your ego's programme and emotional servitude."

"When you say, 'I am what I am and I can't change that', then I say to you that nothing could be further from the truth; you are a biological, physical entity that is seeded with the evolutionary capacity to evolve and transform, just as the caterpillar. Even your science will tell you such truth; your brain is of such a sublime design that you have the capacity through focus and imagination to change its very neuronal structure. Even your DNA is designed to express, or switch off and on different aspects if given the right stimulus from the environment. So you are indeed an entity that is designed for change."

Lilly again interrupted to ask a question, "But if I am an ego that has been programmed deliberately for my soul's development, why do I need to change that, if that seems to produce a physical reality that is my destiny?"

"A wonderful question, my love; the ego is always seeking a reward for its effort and discomforts, as change is not one of the ego's favoured things to do. So let's see if I can convince you that this journey of spiritual enlightenment is well worth the effort."

"Remember I explained to you previously that you are a vibratory being, always broadcasting your state of being into the ether and then attracting back to yourself the likeness of those vibrations. This is how you participate as a co-creator of your physical reality. If you accept this truth, then it reveals the significance that your predominant states of being are your point of attraction."

"Now, what is your state of being you may well ask? Let us imagine your ego as being a grand mansion of multiple 'rooms', where each room contains the memories, beliefs, behaviours and attitudes of a particular emotional state that you have experienced in your past. As soon as a memory is triggered you enter this room and a cascade of neurochemicals starts to be released into your body as peptides, which then creates a feeling in your body that fits with the memory and thinking. You have already experienced what I am talking about, my love, when the vision of your son was replayed to you earlier and your body responded as if the event had just happened. Now, the continual repetition of these rooms being visited over and over again creates a feeling of familiarity for the ego, as it considers this feeling an assurance of its existence and identity. These familiar states of being become so frequently used that they are held in the subconscious and retrieved automatically as reactions and responses to all of the events and circumstances you are confronted with each day. Your programmed emotional events from the past are now creating your present and you are not even consciously aware of it."

"If I talk of addictions of the physical body I know that you understand them in relation to substances such as drugs, caffeine, alcohol or nicotine; however, you are probably totally unaware that your emotions are highly addictive as well, because they have a neurochemical or peptide produced every time you enter that room. This is what I mean by being bound by emotional servitude; you have become addicted to the continual feeding of your physical body with these emotional states of being. When you suffer a loss of a physical entity or through abandonment, the pain and suffering you experience as heartache is the sensual stimuli of that entity no longer being fulfilled; you experience a withdrawal."

"Whenever I talk of chemical addictions, it is remembering that the biochemical nature of your physical garment is subject to homeostasis, always seeking equilibrium of its bodily processes. So when a withdrawal is experienced, your body goes looking for another feast of chemical and draws you back to a memory in your past to get you thinking in such a way that the neuropeptide is again secreted. This is what keeps you locked into your depression and anxiety, feeling as if there is no escape. You are chemically kept in the past, reliving those traumatic events over and over again. Unless you change your habitual way of thinking, then you are forever locked into these states of being that your ego is telling you this is who you are. Your personality and identity are really a habitual attitude."

"If you understand that when you become addicted to your emotional states of your ego, such as ones of feeling guilt and shame, remorse and regret, considering yourself as a victim, being angry and resentful, feelings of lack or unworthiness, then these become your predominant states of being that are continuously being transmitted and broadcasted into the ether. The stronger your emotional states are held over a long period of time, then inevitably there will be events and circumstances manifested into your physical reality, that will be attracted to you as an experience as surely as a magnet pulls towards itself."

"Now, let's consider this a little further and contemplate where do the peptides and other neurochemicals come from? When you delve a little deeper you will see that those 'rooms' of your ego's personality are made up of neuronal synaptic connections joined together like a network of webs. When one starts to fire with an electrical impulse, then so do all of the others linked to it; they become a synchronistic attractor pattern of neuronal firing, drawing the thoughts arising into your level of conscious awareness. This is called associative memory. Every time a neuron fires it produces a neurochemical of information. So you see, my love, you can only ever talk about, think about and perceive sensually to the extent that you have a neuronal synaptic web in place for; this is the boundary of your ego's personality construct or programme. This is close-mindedness because you are limited by your current level of knowledge and past memory that is creating a physical reality within this boundary of what you know."

"When I say you are the alchemist, I am not just speaking metaphorically. To transform your ego's programme by breaking free of your habitual responses and all its associated neurochemicals is indeed a grand transmutation of your inner alchemy. Your heaven and hell dwell in the same temple, as you are the creator of both within your mind. Your emotional states of being are the master's key, my love. To have dominion over your ego's fears and anxieties is to hold within your hand the sceptre of power that has been hidden inside you since the day you were born. This is why I am here, to help you remember this truth that you are a co-creator with the Divine. Fear is the only thing that separates you from your greatest desires and the sublime experience of your dreams of a better day; to become the butterfly."

"To move you to a higher plane of reality, then your ego's fears must be dealt with. There is only one beast that is ever- reliant on you to continually feed it for its existence, that is the 'mangy dog' that knows only fear; the powerful wolf in the forest of abundance needs only itself, for it knows the freedom that dwells within and is never enslaved or tethered by anything external to it."

Lilly asked with curiosity, "How does an emotional state turn into a physical experience then? I thought my emotions were a reaction to something happening to me, rather than the other way around that you are suggesting."

"To answer that beautiful question, my love, you need to venture with me a little bit further down the rabbit hole and turn to some science for your answer, for there lies within the secret of creation."

"At the visible, macro level of your physical reality the Newtonian laws of physics governs the nature of existence, where everything appears separate and distinct from your own individual form. This is the world of your sensual reality, a materialistic perspective where everything is experienced externally to you as individuated solid matter. The survivalist ego perceives objectively from this vantage point and is continuously interacting and relating to this external environment."

"Now, if you delve instead into the micro world of the subatomic realms, science will show you that there is no objective reality; you enter the weird and wonderful world of quantum physics. This is a world of uncertainty, an invisible realm that can only be understood through mathematical equations and theories. The quantum field exists as a dual nature of waves and particles. The electromagnetic waves are vibrating, oscillating, spinning vortices of various frequencies and amplitudes, spread out through the ether. When those waves collapse they become particles; little quanta sized packets of information and energy. It is these particles that are the foundations or building blocks of all matter that your sensory perceptions see and feel as being solid."

"This quantum field is like the womb of creation, because those waves that are radiating, all spread out, can only be described as existing as possibilities of being created. Let me help your understanding by perhaps explaining it this way. Imagine if you will a portrait of the *Mona Lisa*. In the macro world of Newtonian physics you are observing the portrait in its entirety, where you can see the frame surrounding the painting, as well as every detail of her face, her hair and clothing. You come to know this portrait because you see every detail in context and relative to everything around it. Now, if you were to zoom in at a microscopic level of the subatomic realm, all you can know is a blur of paint as a pixel. You have now lost the objective perspective that the portrait offered before; you have no definite understanding or meaning of what you are observing. You could be looking at part of her nose, her hair or her smile; you are filled with uncertainty, which is a feature of the wave function of the quantum field. You know that the entire portrait still exists simultaneously as a possibility, but you are not an objective viewer as before; you are immersed within the portrait itself."

"So how does this wave function existing only as a potential creation collapse into a particle? Quantum physics calls it the 'observer' effect. When you, as the 'observer', want to make known what part of the portrait you are looking at, for example the eye of Mona Lisa, then your intention to measure, or observe and go looking for the eye, then collapses the wave of potential into a definite location in space and time, which is the particle. As each particle or pixel is drawn together in likeness, a picture of the eye starts to emerge into your experience for you to perceive. You could say that the quantum field creates something for you to look at only when you intend to go looking for it."

"In the quantum field you are not a separate or objective part of creation; your consciousness as the observer directly participates in the act of creation itself. Without you everything remains only as a wave of potential of creation; like the Mona Lisa remaining only in the mind of Leonardo da Vinci. Without *you* the consciousness of the divine mind exists only as a potential of creativity; your individuated consciousness is required to bring it out of the invisible realm into the visible manifested realms of your third-dimensional plane to be experienced by your physical bodily garment sensually."

"Now, I am trying to keep this very simple, my love, as quantum physics is a realm of very complex science to understand. But, if you can grasp the concept that everything visible in form to your perceptions arises from an unseen and invisible quantum realm first, then that is a significant understanding. Then further to that, to understand that it takes a participation of consciousness in the role of 'observer', to collapse waves of creative 'possibilities' into manifested particles of existence is also significant. The building blocks to the solid forms perceived on your screen of reality are particles; this is a truth at a fundamental level of science. The cornerstone of creation can then be described as 'consciousness and energy create the nature of reality'. For it takes consciousness as the role of 'observer' to collapse a vibrationary wave of energy into a particle, which are the foundations of all matter. So when I tell you that mind creates matter, you can see that there is a scientific basis for this truth."

"If I take you back to the little neurons of synaptic web connections in your brain's anatomy and zoom in on the inner neuronal cells they are built from, then you would find little, skeletal structures called microtubules. These little structures are so small that they exist at the quantum field level of subatomic particles. The tubules could be imagined as a harp with strings that vibrate at various rates, communicating with the quantum field of 'possibilities'; your body is strumming a tune."

"This is how your physical body communicates your emotional states of being into the quantum field to collapse the wave function into particles. What you are thinking and feeling never stays within the confines of the boundary of your body, but is transmitted and broadcasted into the third- dimensional plane of space and time that is constructing your reality. So I will say to you, my love, what you think and feel matters, because your thoughts are a powerful creative force that creates the physical forms on your screen of reality."

"The feeling of being separated and isolated is an illusion of your brain's anatomy. You are immersed and connected by a sea of consciousness and energy to everything that you visibly perceive and don't see. The waves of the quantum field hold as a divine memory every 'possibility' of creation and every 'probability' that has been created in the past. When you are living only from the ego's limited programme of habitual responses and reactions, then you are playing the same old song over and over again, creating only from the waves of probabilities. If you are able to change your mind, move to a new way of thinking, then you are also creating a new neuronal web of connections and those microtubules start to sing your new tune. If this new tune is persistent, then the quantum field responds by collapsing the waves of creative possibilities and you start to see a whole new reality come into existence; you have changed your life simply by changing your mind. Remember when I said to you before, my love, that just like a caterpillar you are seeded with the ability of transformation."

"This new knowledge may help you understand that when you continue to react to the circumstances that come into your reality on a daily basis, you are reacting to an older version that you have already created and brought into manifestation. You can never change the external reality by continuing to think and behave in the same way and expect something different to happen. A problem created on a lower level of consciousness can never be solved with the same mind or consciousness that created it; a change of mind, an evolution to a higher level of consciousness, is required to permanently resolve your ego's dilemmas. This is where the long, slow vibrations of fear are ascended to the faster vibrational rate of unconditional love. When you can bring yourself to the absolute place of acceptance that you are a co-creator of your reality, that you have created your own demons, only then can you realise if you created a version of hell, then it takes the same energy and process to create heaven."

"What version of the Mona Lisa you see on your screen of reality is dependent on your vibrational broadcast. The lower vibrations of the ego's fear will only allow you to perceive its vibrational equivalent; maybe a fraudulent, poorly painted copy of the original Mona Lisa. If you are instead broadcasting a faster vibrational frequency of love, gratitude, joy and excitement, then the vibrational equivalent will also show up on your screen of reality. You may find yourself in Paris admiring the original work of art on display."

"You see my love, creation is not so much about creating anything, as everything already exists as a possibility in the divine mind. It is more about becoming the vibrational equivalent of what you desire to experience; this is the art of manifestation. Your whole screen of reality that you call life is a feedback mechanism for the soul's development of vibrational energy."

"When you perceive life from this perspective of a vibrational reality, then your experiences may begin to make more sense. In your world of ego perspective it is one of always allowing the external environment to determine your attitudes and states of being; you are always reacting and responding habitually. Life becomes a circle of recreating the same experiences because it cannot create anything different. The human entity has its reality all switched about, it works in opposition to the laws of creation. The mortal looks to external circumstances for reliance on creating its predominant states of being; it doesn't allow itself to be happy and content until the people, places and circumstances fit a certain ideal. The mortal is forever in a state of discontent, believing that when it achieves its desires and wants, such as a loving relationship, new toil or more gold coin for example, only then will it feel peace, security and fulfilment."

"The ego only knows an existence of fear, a need to survive and prosper. So all of its desires are motivated by a perception of lack; that it doesn't yet have what it needs to be safe and secure. So the ego's vibrations of fear and lack are being broadcasted into the ether and, sure enough, all of the circumstances and events equivalent to that level of attraction return as a mirror to that frequency. The entity then experiences itself as a witness to someone else having a loving relationship, someone else getting a promotion or someone else having an abundance of the gold coin they so desperately want. All of the desires of the entity remain unfulfilled and separate from them, because they are a mirror reflection of their state of being which was originally sent. The law of vibration can only manifest into your reality what you are a vibrational match to. To fall in love with your current circumstances, to see the perfection of the divine mind in every creation, to know that you are perfect and loved, that your world is abundant and beautiful, to be peaceful, content and secure, regardless of what your eyes are telling you, that then becomes your point of attraction. When you can see all of the perfection of your reality with the same mind as the divine creator, only then will your desires manifest into a physical reality and be made available to you. That is the challenge, my love."

As the prophet paused, Lilly thought for a moment and then replied with sadness, "I appreciate you telling me all this, I really do; it's all so surreal. But at the heart of everything is that I miss them so much, so, so much. My heart constantly aches. Understanding all the science helps me intellectually, but not in my heart. I just can't switch that off and be some Pollyanna and pretend it didn't happen; just put a smile on my face and get on with it."

The prophet was quick to respond, "I don't for one moment suggest to you that you don't grieve or let yourself feel the loss of the loved ones in your life; for that is your beautiful heart finding its peace. This is why I have let you see aspects of your life and your husband's from the perspective of an observer, to help you find a place to put those events to rest. In many respects the quality of your life will be determined by your ability to let go. I do not mean to cast those memories aside, but not to hold the memory as a way of punishing yourself, by continuously feeling guilty or remorseful; that is what does you the most harm."

"If I can help you by sharing a new perspective on the reality of your life that you have not known before, which then helps you see that your life serves great purpose in the divine plan of creation, then so be it. It is not for you to move from a place of despair to being a Pollyanna, as you refer, in one giant leap. But if you can take a small step from the feeling of hopelessness and move towards at least faith, then that is a giant leap within itself; for in faith you allow yourself to dream the dream of a better day. You see, my love, your broken heart leaves you locked in a room trying desperately to open a door that has been closed to you, believing that it is the only way out. Yet, right beside you is an open door of new possibilities, new dreams, a new life waiting for you to take the first step towards it. As the great Chinese philosopher, Lao-Tzu once beautifully proclaimed, 'A journey of a thousand miles begins with a single step'. If our time spent together helps you at the very least start to move towards that door of faith, then my purpose here is well served."

"Now, there is still much to share with you my love about the nature of your reality, would you like me to continue?" the prophet asked inquisitively.

"Well it's not as if I have anywhere else to be, so please do, I would like to know more," Lilly replied.

"Excellent! Now, I am going to share with you again another image from your past. When I was talking before about the nature of your emotional addictions, I want you to know that your emotional body has the capacity at a subconscious level to find that one person in a million who can feed it. Relationships are founded on the human entity's need for love and connection with another person external to itself. It becomes like two broken hearts searching for their own healing and completeness in the heart of another."

"So once again my love, just watch …..just watch."

CHAPTER 9

Empire, Michigan.
March 2005

As Lilly sat at the reception desk she looked up at the clock on the wall and watched the hand slowly tick over to 7pm; the ticking hand obediently counting down the seconds seemed to stop, bringing the perfect rhythmic noise to a halt. As if playing with her, the hand moved again, continuing on its circular journey, maybe with a little satisfaction at its timely joke.

Still another hour to go, she thought to herself, feeling thoroughly bored as she returned her attention back to the computer screen in front of her on the desk. Lilly read through her email, which was beginning to take on the length of a small novel, and in satisfaction signed off with her familiar love and kisses to her older sister. Just as her finger was primed and ready to push the send button, the door in front of her was whisked open and a rush of cold air entered the cosy office. The figure of a tall, solid man with closely shaved, dark hair wearing faded-blue denim jeans, collared white shirt and a warm brown, suede jacket, entered through the open doorway and now stood there in front of her seated behind the desk. Prompted by his entrance, Lilly bounced to her feet and immediately locked on to the warmest brown eyes she had ever gazed upon; she could feel her heartbeat start to go wild, sending a bizarre tingling feeling rushing through her young, trim body. As if waiting for her to say something, he broke into a smile, which only caused her to melt even more and feel her knees start to go weak.

Lilly fought to bring her racing heart and mind under control and at least say something, instead of standing there like an idiot looking at a dreamy hunk of a man that had somehow miraculously transformed her boredom into a defining moment of heavenly bliss.

"Hi, welcome to the Lakeshore Inn, can I help you?" Lilly finally blurted out, refusing to unlock herself from those dark-brown eyes that were still looking at her.

"Hi, I'm after a room for a couple of nights. I haven't made a booking, so I'm hoping you have something," he replied, still beaming his beautiful smile.

Knowing full well that there were nine of the eleven rooms vacant, Lilly flicked through the pages of the large, green guest ledger in front of her, feigning a serious investigation in answer to his question.

"Hmm …. let me see, I'm pretty sure we have something for you. Yes, room 9 is available for a couple of nights. Is it just yourself?" Lilly asked, turning her attention from the ledger back to Mr Dreamy and those eyes again.
"Yep, just me"

As Lilly's heart skipped a beat yet again with the revelation that Dreamy was out and about all by himself, she retrieved the relevant form from its hiding place on the desk and placed it in front of him.

"Great," she said, with a smile clearly broadcasting her delight at his answer. "If you just fill out your details on this form we can get you settled in."

Lilly watched as a firm hand took the pen and dutifully filled in the form he had been given; taking the opportunity to secretly evaluate Dreamy's muscular frame while he was occupied.

As he finished he turned the form back towards Lilly for her appraisal and pulled a brown wallet from the back pocket of his jeans.

Scanning through the details, Lilly replied, "All the way from Australia, Mr Andaman? You're a long way from home. Have you been touring the States for long?"

"Please, call me Mitch. No, I flew into New York this morning and then onto Travesty and I've driven here this afternoon. I'm not really doing the tourist thing, more of a personal business trip really."

Lilly fought back the overwhelming urge to interrogate him further, not wanting to flatten first impressions like a sledgehammer with being too nosy. Instead she followed her normal, polite script and placed the room key on the desk in front of him.

"Well, I hope you enjoy your stay here. Room 9 is at the end of the ground floor verandah and I'm sure you'll find it clean and comfortable. If there is anything I can do to help, please don't hesitate to ask," Lilly said in a very collected calm voice, whilst secretly inside pleading, *Please ask! … Ask me anything!*"

As she watched him pick up the keys, he remained standing there, not moving, just looking at her. Her mind raced. *Is he going to ask me out? Has he fallen head over heels for me?* She felt like a school-girl with a very big crush.

"Money? How much do you want for the room?" he finally said in a curious tone; after it was obvious that Lilly had clean forgotten about taking payment for the room.

Now feeling even more like an idiot, and a face flushing with embarrassment, Lilly gave a slight laugh in an attempt to cover up her discomfort, "*Oh!* Of course, silly me! That will be $120 for the two nights."

With the smile returning to his face, Mitch handed over the crisp
bills from his wallet and waited patiently while she wrote him a
receipt. As he took it from her, he then turned to open the door and
let himself out. "You have a good night now," he said on his way
out.

"Yes, you too," Lilly said, still feeling flustered and totally
incompetent.

*You idiot! idiot! idiot! Dreamy's going to think you're a complete
moron!* she lambasted herself as she sat back down in the leather
office chair.

Lilly turned her attention back to the email that was still waiting
patiently on the computer screen to be transported along fibre cables
to its destination in Toronto. She couldn't stop thinking about him.
*What a hunk! I wonder what he does for a living? Why is he here in
Empire? Maybe he already has a girlfriend and he's here to visit
her? Maybe he's gay! God I hope not! How old do you think?
Twenty-something? Twenty-five at least! Stop it, stop it, stop it! He's
not interested in you ... obviously!*

Lilly glanced at the clock yet again; time was still dragging despite
her pleasant five-minute interlude. She pushed the send button on the
waiting email and then promptly opened up a new message to start a
fresh one to a friend from College. As she became engrossed in the
screen, typing away yet another small novel of news to her friend,
she jumped as the door opened again, startling her. He was back.

"*Oh!* Hello again, is everything OK?" Lilly inquired, her heart yet
again thumping away inside her chest as he approached her desk.

"I thought maybe you could help me out."

"Absolutely, what do you need?" Lilly replied, hoping not to sound *too* desperate.

Mitch held out towards her a piece of paper with a name and address written on it. "I'm looking for the Point Betsie Lighthouse; apparently Ben and Laura Steiner live there. Do you know them at all?" he asked inquisitively.

"I certainly do. They are caretakers out at the Betsie Lighthouse. You just follow route 22 south towards Frankfort for about 12 miles. Although you might miss the turn-off at this time of night if you're not sure where you are going," Lilly replied with some concern in her voice.

"No, that's OK, I am going to head there tomorrow morning. I was just making sure I   had the right place, that was all."

"Right. They are a lovely couple. They've been out at the lighthouse for a few years now. Have you met them before?" Lilly asked.

"No, I've never met them. I knew their son Richard though."

"Oh! I see," Lilly's mind was racing; whether to make the offer or not. In the end she decided what the heck, just spit it out, "Look, I don't work tomorrow, maybe I could take you down there and introduce you to Ben and Laura, especially if you've come all this way to see them as a friend of Richard's."

"That's really kind of you to offer, but I really don't want to put you out….."

Before Mitch had a chance to even finish Lilly jumped in, "*Really!* It's not putting me out at all. I haven't got any plans for tomorrow, nothing to do at all, so I would love to." By this stage, Lilly really didn't care if she was sounding pushy and in desperate need of a life.

With that smile back again on his face, Mitch gave up all resistance and said, "Well, OK then. I'll meet you out the front at 10, is that OK by you?"

"Fantastic. That will be perfect. Out the front then, OK, cool," Lilly replied nervously.

"Great. Can I know your name, so I can hunt you down if you don't show up?" Mitch
replied with a tone of laughter in his voice.

"*Oh!* Of course, I'm Lilly," she laughed back, thinking to herself, *you can hunt me down anytime you like ...grrr!*

"All right then, Lilly, I'll see you tomorrow." Mitch said as he slowly backed out the door   and was gone again.

"Yep, see you tomorrow Mitch," Lilly replied, again melting at the knees as the sound of his name came rolling off her tongue.

Oh my God! A date with Dreamy! Lilly thought, as her mind raced with the bliss of spending some time with the hunk that had just happened to show up out of the abyss of nowhere. With one last glance of the clock and a smile firmly locked on her pretty young face, Lilly decided it was time to go home and get some beauty sleep; after all, it was a big day tomorrow.

The next morning Lilly drove down Front Street of Empire and pulled into the car park of the Lakeshore Inn; she saw him standing patiently outside on the verandah. She had changed her clothes five times already and meticulously applied her make-up, yet was still filled with nervousness as she flicked her long, brown hair back and checked her eyes quickly in the rear view mirror as he walked towards her car and opened the door. Lilly's heart went into overdrive yet again as he seated himself in the passenger seat next to her.

"Hi Lilly," Mitch said, as he turned to her with a warm smile lighting up his cleanly shaven face.

As the aroma of his aftershave filled the confines of her small car, Lilly thought he smelt as divine as he looked. "Hi Mitch, did you sleep alright?"

"Yep, I was pretty tired, so I slept like a log."

Lilly pulled out of the car park and turned onto Route 22, giving her best impression of being the safest driver in Michigan. With an awkward silence filling the car, Mitch watched as they drove past trees beginning their return to spring and regrowth of fallen leaves. Some unmelted clumps of snow lined the highway.

"It's a nice part of the world you live in. Have you lived here long?" Mitch finally asked to break the silence.

"Yes, I've lived here all my life. It's really pretty this time of year but it gets cold in winter when the snow comes in. Do you get snow where you live?" Lilly asked, trying to share the conversation.

"Not in Perth there isn't, but if you go east there are some great snow resorts. Perth gets
hot rather than cold."

As Lilly drove they shared a casual banter back and forwards about the weather and the tourist sites of their respective home towns, not delving into anything too personal. By the time Lilly reached the turn-off and indicated to turn right she was feeling a lot more relaxed; he seemed a really nice guy, she thought. The sound of his Australian accent just melted her heart every time he spoke.

The site of the Lighthouse heralded their arrival and Lilly parked the car. "Here we are," she said, just in case it wasn't perfectly obvious to Mitch that they had reached their destination.

As Mitch stepped out of the car he stood for a moment and took in the majestic site of the lighthouse perched proudly on the beach-front, looking longingly out onto the vast Lake Michigan. The lighthouse backed comfortably on to a two-story building with four wood- trimmed window frames perched high on the red roof. The lower level was white-painted brick with steps leading up to a small porch near the door. A flag pole stood nearby with the US flag flapping away in the cool morning breeze.

"Wow!" said Mitch, sincerely impressed by what he was looking at. "What a great lighthouse. I can't say I've seen anything quite like this one."

"She's beautiful isn't she?" Lilly replied, as if she herself was personally responsible for such a grand design being brought into existence. "Lake Michigan has heaps of lighthouses, but I think this is one of the best."

Lilly began walking towards the lighthouse entrance and Mitch stepped up behind her whilst still admiring his surroundings and the vastness of the lake. As Lilly reached the wooden door, she knocked firmly and then turned to smile at Mitch as they patiently waited for any answer. The door opened and a woman wearing a warm jumper and black slacks stood there. Her short, wavy-brown hair tinged with grey framed a soft face that immediately burst forth into a smile at the recognition of Lilly on her doorstep.

"*Lilly!* How lovely to see you, what are you doing out this way?" the woman replied in a genuine delight at seeing Lilly, whilst also curiously eyeing off Mitch standing next to her.

"Hi Laura. I've brought a friend of Richard's to see you; he's come all the way from Australia to see you and Ben."

"*Oh my!* Of course, come in. Please, both of you come in," Laura replied, opening the door wider and ushering them inside to the warmth of her home.

"Laura, this is Mitch Andaman," Lilly said confidently, taking charge of introductions.

Mitch stepped forward and held out his hand, "Nice to meet you, ma'am."

Totally ignoring his outstretched hand, Laura stepped towards Mitch and hugged him in a loving embrace as a mother would have done to a long-lost son. "It's nice to meet you, Mitch; Richard spoke very highly of you in his letters," she said.

Finally, reluctantly releasing him from her hold, Laura stepped back a little flustered at her   outpouring of affection. "Come into the living room and I'll go and find Ben," she said, at the same time leading them to a small living room off to the left.

As Laura disappeared, Lilly made herself comfortable on the floral couch with a window at her back and watched Mitch. It was silent except for the ticking of a clock on the wall. After pausing for a minute, Mitch walked towards a wooden crafted sideboard displaying framed photographs. Neatly folded in a triangle shape rested an American flag. He lightly touched the cloth of the flag and let his hand rest for a moment, not saying anything. He then picked up a framed photograph of a portrait of a uniformed marine, with medals and insignia proudly displayed across the crisp, starched uniform. The smiling face of Richard beamed back at him under the black, shiny peak of a white military cap. As he put the framed photo back down, his eyes perused through the others standing on display. A family shot of the three of them; Richard holding a baseball bat; father and son in a hug; a school graduation photo and another one of a shirtless son on top of an army tank, wearing sunglasses. Mitch felt his chest start to tighten.

"Are you OK?" Lilly asked him in concern.

Before he had a chance to reply, an older man with greying hair walked into the room with a big smile looking first to Mitch and then to Lilly. "Hello people, how are you, Lilly? Great to see you again," he said, as he walked over to Lilly, who stood to retrieve a warm hug.

Turning towards Mitch, Lilly said, "Ben, I would like you to meet Mitch Andaman. He's from Australia."

As Ben walked towards Mitch, he took a firm grip on his hand and shook it vigorously, "Nice to meet you at last Mitch. My boy thought of you as a brother, so I'm proud to have you in my home."

"Thank you, Sir," Mitch replied, as he looked at a face and smile that was so similar to the cheeky grin that his mate had. The resemblance made his chest tighten even more.

"Please have a seat, both of you. Laura's just making a pot of tea, so she'll be out shortly," Ben urged as he perched himself on the twin couch closest to where he was standing.

"So, have they still got you in Afghanistan, Mitch?" Ben asked, turning to Mitch who was now seated on a single couch.

107

Lilly listened on attentively as Ben was now undertaking her desired interrogation of Mitch. *Bless him*, she thought.

"I flew out a couple of days ago to head home. But I've come via the States as I have
something for you both that I promised Ric I would deliver personally."

Ben's eyebrows lifted in surprise and curiosity as he edged forwards on the couch. Before he had a chance to respond though, Laura walked into the lounge room carrying a tray of morning tea for her guests.

As she placed the tray down on the coffee table, she said in a delighted voice, "This is so nice, we don't get many visitors other than tourists this time of year."

"Love, Mitch has come all this way to give us something from Richard," Ben said to Laura as she sat down next to him on the couch.

With all three of them now looking attentively towards Mitch, he reached inside his jacket pocket and retrieved the envelope tucked inside. As he handed it to Ben, he quickly followed with, "I'm sorry it has some dirt on it, but Ric had it on him out in the field. He asked me to bring it to you if something happened to him. I'm so sorry to both of you for your loss. You should be very proud; he was a fine soldier and it was an honour to serve with him."

Ben gently ripped the envelope open and pulled out the pages contained within it. He looked lovingly at his wife seated next to him and then over at Mitch to say, "If you don't mind I would like to read it out loud, as I know Richard thought of you as family; so he would have wanted you to hear these words as well."

As Mitch nodded his head in understanding, Ben started to read;

Dear Mum and Dad,

I'm sorry if you're reading this right now
since it means I didn't make it home.
I hope I made you proud, that's all I've ever
wanted in my life. So if I have left you both
a proud heart and a ton of good memories,
then everything is worth the price.
I loved my country and if you get to live
your freedom at the Betsie, greeting every
stranger with a smile and a cup of tea, then
that's what I went to war to ensure; to
guarantee you and everyone that freedom.
I'm not big on words as you both know, but
I recently read a poem of sorts by a man
named Emerson. It struck a chord with me
so I have included it here to share with
you.

Success

To laugh often and much.

To win the respect of intelligent people and the affection of children.

To earn the appreciation of honest critics and endure the betrayal of

false friends.

To appreciate beauty, to find the best in others,

to leave the world a bit better, whether by a healthy child,

a garden patch or a redeemed social condition;

To know even one life has breathed easier because you have lived.

This is to have succeeded.

I hope in my own small way I have helped
some people breathe a little easier, maybe
brought some hope into their lives where
there wasn't any before. So I know my life
was a success, I know I did you proud and
that's all you ever needed from a son.

I love you both, always remember that.
God bless,
Richard.

When Ben finished reading, he turned to his weeping wife next to him, and held her tightly in a loving, silent embrace. As Lilly watched on, her own memories of Sophia and Phuket flooded into her mind, triggered by the poignant moment; her eyes filled with tears, unable to control the welling emotions any longer.

Mitch felt the familiar return of a churning in his guts and the slight tremble in his body, his eyes locked firmly on his hands held in front of him, not able to look at the sombre scene confronting him. This is the moment he had dreaded, thought about, feared, where the reality of a decision made in a billionth of a second had finally revealed its consequences. Like a ripple on a pond, his choice had transcended the battlefield, the confines of a country's border and journeyed half-way round the world to arrive at this moment in time. He didn't know what to say, the silence was screaming at him, Richard was screaming at him, *"Target confirmed ..Send it! Send it! Send it!"*

Ben finally spoke, pulling Mitch out of a spiralling descent into the darkness of his reminiscence, bringing his awareness back to the warmth of a room, back to a lighthouse in Michigan, back to Lilly looking at him, back to his tormented now.

110

"Mitch! Mitch! Are you all right?" Ben said looking at him with concern.

Mitch looked at him, struggling to come back, struggling to make sense of what he was looking at. Finally, as if having found safe ground to land on, he looked at Ben,
"Yeah…yeah…. I'm OK ….. I'm sorry. Sometimes I get lost."

As Mitch turned to look at Lilly sitting opposite him, their eyes locked together, not saying a word. Lilly could feel him, could feel right through him to every cell in his body. His brown eyes mirrored back to her, his heart mirrored back to her, his pain so obvious mirrored back to her. In that moment she knew, she knew who he was, she 'got' him; and in that very moment she knew with absolute certainty in her heart that she was in love; so madly, so completely, so divinely in love.

Looking to change the dark mood that had seeped in quietly and cloaked the moment, Ben stood up and said to Mitch, "Why don't we let the ladies have a chat and a cup of tea, I want to show you something Mitch."

As Ben walked out to the kitchen with Mitch following, he stopped at the fridge and on opening the door retrieved two beers. "It's probably a bit early in the morning, but I think we could both do with one," Ben said handing a bottle to Mitch.

Screwing the top off, Mitch took a drink and then continued to follow Ben out towards the back and through a wooden door and passageway leading to a spiralling staircase.
 Following Ben up the winding metal staircase, they came to the top of the lighthouse and its circular expanse of glass windows overlooking the lake. The sparkling clean lamp rested in the centre. They both stood next to each other, beers in hand, looking out at the lake.

"Just beautiful, isn't it?" Ben said with a contented sigh in his voice.

"It is. Do you have to light the lamp each evening?" Mitch asked.

"No, no, she's been fully automated since '83. I just do the caretaker's job, a bit
of cleaning and maintenance really, nothing too hard. Richard loved it up here. If
we had a spat or he got upset over something, this is where I'd find him," Ben replied with a chuckle in his voice.

Mitch thought for a moment and then began to say, "Sir, there are some decisions I made in Afghanistan that I ....."

"It's OK, Mitch, you don't have to justify yourself to me or anyone. You did your duty just like Richard did and I'm equally proud of both of you. War is war and crazy things happen; that's just the way it is. We send you boys and gals over there and expect you to do things that no politician would do themselves, then back you come and have to make sense of it all. It's a crazy world at times that even I don't understand."

Pausing for a moment, Ben turned and looked at Mitch, "It means a lot to me and Laura that you came all this way to bring that letter home to us. So thank you, Mitch ..... and stop calling me Sir; you're family now so call me Ben. If there is anything I can ever do for you son, just ask, OK?"

Mitch nodded and thought for a moment before saying, "Thank you Ben, I appreciate that. Can you tell me where you buried him?"

"We laid him to rest at Arlington. Section 60, row 123. He would have wanted to be buried with his colleagues; he loved the Marines despite all the risks. My boy had courage I know that."

After a few moments, Ben broke the silence again and said, "Well we should get back to the girls and see if any of those shortbread biscuits are left; Laura bakes every day, so they are fresh, you'll love them."

As Ben started to descend the stairs, Mitch took one last look at the lake and then followed him. They entered the lounge room to find Lilly and Laura together on the couch with tea cups in their hands, chatting away.

"Oh good, you're both back. Mitch will you and Lilly stay for lunch? It would be lovely to have you stay a little longer?" Laura said looking towards Mitch and back at Lilly in hopeful expectation.

"Sure, that would be nice," Mitch replied as Lilly sat there nodding.

As Laura promptly set off to the kitchen with her new task of preparing lunch in mind, Mitch sat down next to Lilly on the comfortable couch and settled in for the stay.

By the time mid-afternoon had arrived, with stomachs full of lunch and conversation having reached its, limits Mitch and Lilly commenced their warm goodbyes to their generous hosts. With the last waves of goodbye, Lilly wound up the car window and headed back towards the highway and Empire, delighted to have Mitch all to herself at last.

Looking briefly across at Mitch as she drove, Lilly said, "That must have been really hard for you to do. You have a beautiful heart you know."

"Well a promise is a promise to mates. I wish I was here under different circumstances, but that's just the way it is," Mitch replied sombrely.

"Would you like to come with me to the tavern and we could have a drink and a laugh together … cheer you up a bit. What do you think?" Lilly suggested, with a cheeky grin on her face.

"Sure, why not? I could do with a drink."

"Cool," Lilly replied as her heart started to go into overdrive all over again.

As Lilly rapidly completed the drive back to Empire, no longer concerned with any impressions of being the safest driver, she parked the car and led Mitch towards the tavern entrance. As they entered the tavern, Mitch took in the surroundings of wood-panelled walls and round tables with groups of people laughing and enjoying Friday afternoon drinks. A sign reading, Joe's Friendly Tavern hung on the wall above the bar, next to neat lines of empty beer bottles on display. Approaching the bar, a large bearded man in red flannelette shirt stood behind the counter and smiled as they walked towards him, wiping a glass in the process.

"Hey Lilly, what can I get you?" he asked with a warm smile on his face.

"Hi Jimmy. I'd like you to meet a friend of mine, Mitch," Lilly said proudly, showing off her brand new acquaintance.

After a vigorous handshake between the two and a bit of teasing over the fact Mitch was an Aussie, they finally settled with drinks in hand at a wooden booth near the window.

"Well, this is nice," Lilly said, taking a sip from her glass of Coors beer and eager to continue with the interrogation of the handsome hunk that Ben had started.
"So tell me, how long have you been in the military?"

"About six years, since I was nineteen. I've been with the SAS Regiment in Perth
for the last three years, which has been interesting. I've always wanted to be in the Army. My dad was in the US Navy so that influenced me."

With her curiosity now well peaked, Lilly asked, "So how did you end up in Perth with a dad in the US Navy?"

Mitch laughed, "It's a bit of a romance story really. My dad was serving on the *USS Enterprise,* which docked in Fremantle and he met my mum; they fell in love and she ended up following him around the world until she got pregnant with me in '79. So my mum and dad got married and I was born in Denver."

"Wow, you're an American Australian, lucky you," Lilly laughed, taking another sip of her beer.

"Yeah, I suppose I am. Not that I remember much about the States. Mum was homesick after having me, so Dad quit the Navy and they moved back to Perth to be around her family. My brother Christopher was born after me and we grew up in the Hills. It was a good life, a great place to grow up near the bush."

"So do you have to go back to Afghanistan again?" Lilly asked, inwardly hoping that he would say no, not wanting him to end up like his friend and leave her with a broken heart.

Mitch paused and took a drink from his glass of Scotch, not sure of his answer. "I'm due back at the Regiment in a couple of days. I've just done a nine-month tour, so I have some leave owing. After that, if we go back, I'm not sure; time will tell. But anyway, enough of me, tell me all about you; what does a beautiful young woman like yourself do in this little town, apart from hanging out at the tavern on a Friday night?"

Lilly laughed, still thinking he was absolutely gorgeous. "Well, let me see. I was born and raised in Empire. My folks are now retired in Florida, enjoying the sunshine. My older sister, Olivia, lives in Toronto with her husband and twin children. I've been at Northwestern Michigan College for the last two years, but I just started the job at the Lakeshore Inn last month. So you were lucky to run into me yesterday, normally I would be at college."

"Well, lucky me! So what are you studying at college?" Mitch asked with curiosity.

"I'm doing a teaching degree. I love history, so I would like to teach it to children one day."

"Why aren't you still studying then?"

"Um, I needed a break; I couldn't really focus on study at the moment. I was in Phuket over Boxing Day and I lost my best friend Sophia, in the tsunami; so I just can't do it at the moment." Lilly said quietly as the thought of her friend returned yet again.

Sensing her unease, Mitch reached over and gently took hold of her hand, "I'm really sorry to hear that, it must have been really tough. At least you made it out alive."

Lilly squeezed his hand back and gave him a smile, not wanting the situation to deteriorate into one of gloom and doom. "Do you know what is really strange? Your surname is the name of the sea that hit Phuket …. the Andaman Sea. How's that for a coincidence?"

"Really," replied Mitch with genuine surprise. "Do you know what else is really bizarre? Richard died on the same day as your friend, Boxing Day. It's crazy when you think about what it took for us to meet, very crazy, huh?"

As they both looked into each other's eyes, their connection grew in intensity at the realisation of their shared experience in the loss of a loved friend. Mitch squeezed her hand a little tighter.

"Maybe I'm here to tell you to get that hot little butt of yours back to college. I think that's what Sophia would have wanted you to do, hey?" Mitch said with concern.

"I'm sure I will, but maybe just not this year. I've always wanted to write a novel, so perhaps I'll give that a try for a while as a distraction; something different. Or maybe I'll just hop on an aeroplane with you tomorrow and follow you around like a lovesick puppy like your mum did with your dad," Lilly offered with some humour to lighten the moment.

"Babe, I'm probably not the sort of guy you want to get hooked on; I come with a lot of baggage, you know. If war has taught me anything, it's to live each day in the moment, enjoy what you have, laugh when you can and take each day as a gift because it could be your last. So what's say we do just that tonight, enjoy our time together, no strings attached, just have a good time."

Lilly smiled and held her glass of beer up to lightly touch Mitch's Scotch glass, "Cheers to that Mitch and 'cheers' to absent friends who brought us together even for just one day, God bless them."

CHAPTER 10

The beeping sound of the alarm on the clock radio next to the bed drew a reluctant Lilly out of her deep slumber and dream. Through squinting eyes she looked at the red digital display of 7am shining at her.

"Uhhh! You've got to be kidding," she said out loud as her hand reached over to press the top button on the clock to stop the annoying beeping sound.

Resting her head back on the soft white pillow, she slowly realised she wasn't in her own bed. Lilly propped herself up on her elbows, turned on the bedside lamp and looked around the motel room with her clothes scattered on the floor. A memory of the night before finally wound its way through the fogginess of her early-morning mind and a smile emerged to light up her face.

Lilly pulled herself up to a sitting position on the bed and saw the light peeping under the door of the ensuite and heard the sound of running water. Rising slowly out of bed, she turned on the light and picked up her crumpled clothes off the floor and dressed herself. As she stood there looking at the packed duffle bag, the ensuite door opened and Mitch appeared, wiping a towel across his handsome face.

"Hey! Sleeping Beauty is awake," Mitch joked at her.

"Who sets an alarm for 7am, for heaven's sake?" Lilly said as she walked towards him.

"My flight leaves in a couple of hours, babe, so I have to get going," Mitch said as he embraced her in a warm hug and then kissed her long and tenderly.

Lilly couldn't pull away; she couldn't tolerate the thought that this was it; he was walking out of her life just as quickly as he had shown up. Her heart was already aching.

Lost in the hug, Mitch said quietly, "You're so beautiful, I'm sorry I have to go. Keep moving on with your life, babe; never let anything stop you from that, hey?"

Lilly pulled back and stood there looking into his eyes. She touched his face softly with her hand and let it rest there, feeling him for the last time and saying, "Well, you take care. Look after that precious heart of yours."

Finally releasing the tender hold on each other, Mitch picked up his bag and opened the door. As Lilly followed him out, she watched as he placed the bag on the back seat of his hire car and then climbed into the driver's seat. Watching him reverse the car, he drove off, giving a small wave as he turned onto the highway and disappeared out of her life.

Mitch watched her in the rear view mirror as he drove off, a lonely figure standing on the verandah waving, watching him go. He felt like a real ass. *Love 'em and leave 'em* he thought to himself, *is that the sort of guy you are?* Mitch had a small war going on in his mind as he drove towards Travesty and his flight out to Washington. He couldn't stop thinking about her; he had let himself feel some sort of emotion for the first time in a long time. He had let himself be loved by someone; it was a strange feeling, not one he was used to.

His six years in the military had taught him a lot about never getting attached to anything; especially people and places. His only friends were work colleagues, as he could never talk about his work with others; remaining aloof and distant was his trademark, what he did best. *I shoot people for a living,* never made for good party conversation, he thought, as people always wanted to know every grizzly detail. It was easier just not to say anything, to keep to himself and let people ride in and out of his life. *No strings attached,* isn't that what he had told Lilly. *Fuck! What an ass,* he thought to himself yet again.

Mitch was comfortable around airports; checking in, collecting baggage, pretending to sleep so that he didn't have to partake in idle conversation with the passenger next to him. He knew all the tricks. He was a seasoned traveller. The trip to Travesty and on to his flight was hassle-free. As the plane took off, he looked out of the window as Michigan faded from view. Thoughts of Lilly filled his mind as he closed his eyes, allowing the memory of the previous night to flood him once again.

By the time the plane landed and he had grabbed his duffle bag off the luggage conveyor belt at the Ronald Regan National Airport in Washington, he felt relaxed and ready for the next part of his journey. After this, he was looking forward to heading home.

Walking out the sliding doors, Mitch hopped in to one of the multiple yellow taxi-cabs patiently waiting for a fare.

"Arlington Cemetery, thanks mate," he said to the driver as he hopped into the back seat of the cab.

"Sure thing, bro'," the young driver said, starting to pull out, whilst looking at his passenger in the rear view mirror. "Are you Australian, bro'?" the driver asked in curiosity.

"Yep," Mitch replied, looking out the window, wishing he had a dollar coin for every time someone asked him that question.

"Arlington, hey? You got brothers there, mate?" he persisted, trying to sound a little Australian like his passenger.

Mitch looked at the young dark eyes looking at him in the mirror, "Yep, a lot of brothers, mate," he replied before looking away again.

Taking the hint that Mitch didn't really want to talk, the driver was content to let the conversation end and turned the radio up.

After a thought, Mitch asked, "Do you reckon you could find a liquor store on the way? I need a couple of things."

"Sure thing, there's a store just up here," the driver replied, as he gradually maneuvered his cab towards the right side of the road and then double-parked to let his passenger out.

As Mitch hopped out of the cab, the driver waited patiently while totally ignoring the tooting drivers behind him. Re-emerging from the store, Mitch carried a blue bag containing a six-pack of beer and a sandwich, which he placed in his bag on the seat next to him.

The cab slowly pulled back out, continuing on with its journey. Mitch continued looking out the window as a scene of the Pentagon came into view; he imagined how many decisions had been made in that building alone that had impacted on his own life, let alone millions of others. The words of his captain came clearly into his mind, *"We have orders to blast the compound with the AT-4…… Base wants a PID."* He knew all of their orders came direct from the Pentagon. His stomach churned again. How ironic, he thought, that some of the human consequences of those decisions, made in the luxury and comfort of an office thousands of miles away, lay in graves just a few hundred feet across the

Boulevard.

As the cab made its way off the highway and turned left into Memorial Drive, the driver spoke again, breaking into Mitch's thoughts, "You want Section 60 bro'?"

"Yeah, thanks," Mitch replied, thinking that the cabbie must be a mind reader, or just plain used to taking thousands of passengers to this site every year.

The cab meandered through the cemetery as Mitch looked at rows upon rows of white marble headstones, until the cab finally stopped at the road's edge.

"Did you want me to wait?" the driver asked, with his arm resting on the seat as he turned to look at Mitch.

Handing the driver a couple of crisp bills, Mitch replied, "No thanks, mate, I might be a while."

As Mitch started walking along the lush green grass he was surrounded by thousands of white headstones. He had never stepped foot on this sacred ground before, but he could feel the sombre energy of the place. It was like nothing he had ever experienced in the past; goose bumps broke out over his arms and he felt a chill run up his spine.

After some minutes walking, Mitch finally found himself at the base of the white headstone he had been looking for. He read the words neatly inscribed in black on the white marble surface.

RICHARD BENJAMIN

STEINER

CPL

US MARINE CORPS

JUL 23 1980

DEC 26 2004
AFGHANISTAN

Mitch placed his bag on the ground and sat down on the lush,
green grass facing the headstone. He looked around and observed
groups of people strolling through the rows and others sitting at
headstones, just as he was. He pulled two bottles of beer out of
his bag, along with his sandwich. On placing one bottle next to
the headstone, Mitch then opened his own and took a gulp of beer,
followed by a bite of his sandwich.

"Cheers, buddy, I finally bought you that beer I owed you," he
said, raising his bottle slightly.

"I did what you asked, mate, I took your letter out to your folks.
It's a nice place where they live, in the lighthouse, really nice."

"You broke their heart mate ….. You broke their heart….. They
liked your letter though….. you wrote them a great letter."

"Your mum's a great cook; she fed us up big time. I took a chick
named Lilly with me bro'…. *Fuck!* You never told me you had
some talent where you lived…. she was *really* beautiful….It was
a hard one leaving her behind."

Mitch went silent for a few moments, thinking of Lilly yet again,
until turning his attention back to the headstone.

"Mate, I never did get to say I'm sorry… so, I'm telling you that
now OK? I'm so fucking sorry. I should have taken that shot and
then we would have been out of there. But no, I played it safe,
took too long to make a fucking decision … a decision that
you've paid for with your life, mate. Now, I have to live with that
every single day… every day I think about it, mate… I picture

123

myself taking the shot....imagining myself taking that shot...knowing that you would still be here if I had just done that."

"I don't know if I can do it anymore .... I just don't know how I'm going to do it....They are going to send me back. The Regiment's going back later this year bro'. So how the fuck am I going to do that when I just can't see the point of it anymore? How am I going to do that...huh? *Fuck!*

"I'm thinking of pulling the pin, mate.... Do one last tour and then move on and do something else...time for a change, maybe...... Yeah! Yeah! I know what you would say...call me a fucking pussy, a weak bugger...but I've had enough mate....I've had enough of war for one lifetime."

Mitch sat there, eating his sandwich and thinking about everything that had happened, not quite knowing what to say anymore. Then he said out loud, "But anyway, bro', I'm going to shoot off now. I've got a flight out this arvo ...I'm going home... so I just wanted to bring you that beer... that's all.... I think about you, mate ... I fucking miss you, you lousy yank..... Just know I'm sorry, mate....I'm sorry ....that's all."

Mitch picked himself off the grass, grabbed his bag, took one last look at the headstone and gave a salute, "See ya, bro'."

Walking slowly back towards the main entrance, a certain peace settled over him. At least he had finally fulfilled the promise made to his friend, to deliver the letter. As he walked the thoughts of Lilly flooded back into his mind. He couldn't stop thinking about her. He thought about what he had said to her. *"Keep moving on with your life babe, never let anything stop you from doing that."* Keep moving on, he thought, just keep moving.

When he reached the main visitor's centre, Mitch looked for a pay phone. He located the crumpled receipt in his pocket, looked for the number he needed and then inserted the coins and dialled. As he patiently waited for an answer, he watched the numerous people in a sombre mood milling around. At last the phone was answered as he heard a male voice on the other end of the line say, "Lakeshore Inn, can I help you?"

"I was wondering if I could speak to Lilly, please?" Mitch asked.

"I'm sorry but she's not working today; can I take a message?"

Mitch's mind raced with whether to leave a message or not and then replied, "No, no that's OK, I'll try again another time." He then placed the handset back down on its cradle.

Standing there for a few moments, Mitch started to move towards a yellow cab parked on the roadside outside. As he hopped in the back seat, he again gave instructions to the waiting cabbie, "Washington Airport, thanks mate."

Watching out the window as the cab moved off, Mitch thought to himself, *time to keep moving... time to go home.*

CHAPTER 11

With Lilly still watching, the prophet began his transformation from one of a screen upon the well wall back to a holographic form in front of her. His beautiful dark eyes once again locked with her own, as Lilly spoke.

"This is so crazy. It feels like I am watching a movie of my life, yet seeing scenes that I was never aware of before. I never realised Mitch carried that much guilt about the death of his friend. When they read that letter, I could see him change inside though. I could feel this grief come to the surface; it was like the same grief I carried in my own heart after losing Sophia and something just 'clicked' inside me."

The prophet listened to Lilly and then responded lovingly, "Ah! Yes, the emotion of guilt is very powerful indeed. Now, here is something for you to understand, my love, every emotion is a continuum of degrees, carrying itself on a spectrum of extremes; this is the law of polarity and it is behind the duality of your third-dimensional plane of existence. Just like a swing of the pendulum, every circumstance and event is being drawn into reality with equal measure of compensation; it is in a constant swing of momentum seeking harmony and balance. So, your emotions are always seeking this balance through your relationships."

"To help you understand this idea a little better, let me turn your mind to the beauteous words written by your Master Shakespeare in centuries past, that say:
All the world's a stage,
And all the men and women merely players,
They have their exits and their entrances,
And one man in his time plays many parts.
126

"You see, these words foretell the wisdom that your reality is indeed much like a grand stage, a platform upon which you create your circumstances and events called life for the very purpose of evoking emotions. Each 'player' appears in your life to provoke and reveal to you an aspect of your ego shadow that is out of tune with your divine essence. Much of your ego's programme lies hidden within your subconscious, beyond your awareness. Instead, you are left to feel the effects of this filter, revealing itself upon the stage of life and the relationships you are drawn to, whereby they play themselves out; to *reveal* themselves to you so to speak."

"Now let us consider the guilt that your husband has immersed himself in through the circumstances of his life events. Guilt is an extreme version of what could be considered as taking full responsibility for what happens in his life; perhaps much like an archetype of a 'martyr'. The great burden of responsibility is carried proudly on his shoulders like a badge of honour, regardless of whether other circumstances or effects may have contributed to a particular outcome or cause. Your husband has chosen to take full responsibility for the death of his friend, despite being caused by means other than his own hand; as this feeds his emotion of guilt. Then there were his thoughts that day when you met and then had to depart, once again luring him into an emotion of guilt at his treatment of you; a *love 'em and leave 'em* attitude, was that not his thought? When it came to the death of your son, his guilt at having purchased the kite that contributed to your son's demise was projected on to yourself, as he was unable to carry the total burden of such an immense load; this is an ego defence and strategy to protect itself. Did your husband not say to you, '*It was your responsibility to keep him safe?*' and also, '*Richie trusted you to do that for him*'? Were they not his words? When you understand that these same words were thought by your husband a thousand times when contemplating his friend's death, then you will come to understand that those words were never intended for you, but for himself."

"That day at the lighthouse when the letter was read you could see and feel those deep feelings of guilt that your husband was experiencing. Your subconscious connected to him because you had carried the same emotion after the death of your own friend. You had found your bedfellow of emotional connection."

"Now, my love, let us swing the pendulum across to its other extreme, for the martyrdom of guilt must have its counterpart within the continuum swing of expression. For the 'martyr' to exist there must be a victim, a person who, unlike the martyr, takes no responsibility. The victim plays the game of blame, dispensing all responsibility to external circumstances. The victim feels totally disempowered to events perceived as beyond their control; a subjugation to people and circumstances who rally their feelings of powerlessness and victimhood. A victim will find itself in circumstances like natural disasters, accidents, criminal acts and victimisation by others, including their rejection and abandonment. They perceive life as a great conspiracy of control dramas, even to the level of government manipulation or cosmic events attributed to acts of God."

"From the very moment your mother spoke those words to you, *the hardest thing about life is living it*, she seeded within you the ego's programme of victim. From the moment your lover walked away saying, *no strings attached*, you knew deep down inside you had found the one person that would one day leave you; just like your friend who was washed away and the passing of your son. Does not your wound of a cross, embedded on your wrist, symbolise the self-proclaimed abandonment of your God? You have played the victim for the largest part of your life. It is what has propelled you to the ultimate thought of suicide; the final act of victim in the drama on your grand stage of life."

"At least the walls of this well visibly reveal to you the prison that holds you here. Your ego instead, has held you in a prison that has never been visible or known to you. It has fed you with an illusion of fear like the 'mangy dog'; denying you knowledge of your true power that is the 'wolf' in the forest of abundance. You are not a victim, you are an unlimited, powerful divine being. The hardest part of your spiritual journey is to turn around and face this truth, to take full responsibility for your creations. Not as the martyr of guilt, for that is a need of the ego, but as a powerful co-creator dwelling in the supreme mind of the Creator. This is who you truly are."

"All of the 'players' on your grand stage of life, with their entrances and exits, play their roles to perfection, to guide you on your great quest to '*know thyself*', to seek the divine treasure within you that I speak of. The 'play' is a masquerade indeed, as your ego is the mask you wear, hiding your true self and cloaked in limitations, pretending to be someone that you are not. This game you play within your relationships is designed to reveal your mask and bring you to the point of revelation of your true divine nature. That is your destiny and purpose; a return to your powerful, complete, perfect, whole and integrated state of being in alignment with the divine creator; an absolute state of 'at-one-ment'."

Contemplating what the prophet had said, Lilly replied, "What you say is very confronting; I have never considered myself as a victim or Mitch as being a martyr. I did the best I could in my life and I have never intended to hurt anyone or play a game, as you suggest."

"As I have said to you before, my love, the spiritual journey takes enormous courage as your very belief about your identity will challenge your ego that fights very hard to keep that identity sustained. I am not saying in any way that you have intended anything, as the core of your beliefs are secreted within your subconscious, outside your awareness. In many respects you are like an iceberg, where only the very tip of existence is above the surface. Lying underneath the waterline is a vast expanse of unseen ice exerting its presence on that which is above it. As you rise and ascend in consciousness and vibration, this very ice below the waterline is pushed to the surface into your awareness to be dealt with and released. All change comes with this awareness as being the first step; for you cannot change what you don't know about yourself. So trust in this part of your journey, as what I confront you with is to assist you with this change."

"All of your emotions serve as a tuning fork, to provide feedback where the pendulum has swung too far to the extreme and you are out of balance and harmony with your natural, divine state of being. Negative emotions, such as anger, shame, guilt, sadness and fear, are simply resistance to your true nature; you are swimming against the tide. They are calls for you to pay attention, to be aware that you have given a circumstance or event a meaning or belief that is not serving you. Remember that your beliefs propel your emotional states of being, or the 'rooms' of the mansion that I spoke about earlier and hence are creating your point of attraction. Beliefs are a very powerful creative force in your life and are the turning point of change. Truly, if the mortal being ever came to understand the creative power of the beliefs in their life they would never stop for one day until every last one is revealed, cast out and seeded anew. For they are what the alchemist casts into the chalice and labours long and arduously until the fire of change births a new golden age and you are born again."

When the prophet paused for a moment, Lilly asked, "I think I understand what you are saying, but I would also like to know more about the law of polarity that you referred to earlier, that sounds very intriguing."

"Indeed, the law of polarity is an essential understanding of the nature of your reality; so let us venture further still down the rabbit hole and see where it takes us. Let me draw into your mind an image of a grand circle. This circle is representative of the divine mind as I explained to you previously. This circle is complete unto itself, it is whole and absolute, at a complete state of fulfilment and rest; it is the 'All', a perfect state of being. Now once again, let's place a dot in the centre of the circle as being representative of the first word or thought of the Divine to 'Exist'. From this dot, let's imagine a plumb line running downwards as a pendulum. This plumb line can be considered as the ripple of energy emanating from the divine mind as vibrational waves. Because this energy is an electrical flow, it is always accompanied by a magnetic field spinning perpendicular to the electric current; they travel together through space as these waves of electromagnetic radiation. So from the very first thought of the divine mind there is a law of polarity created because of this electromagnetic field."

"Let's now consider this plumb line as being representative of the involution or descent of energy I spoke about earlier. Starting from the dot in the circle, this can be called the zero point, as the rate of vibration is so fast it appears to be at rest. Imagine now tying six little pieces of string to the plumb line at neat intervals, ending with the solid pendulum itself. Each piece of string is where the vibrational energy is slowed in frequency and becomes a particular expression of this electromagnetic spectrum. So slowing the waves down to the first string can be called gamma rays, slowing down again to the second string is x-rays, slowing again is ultra-violet blue, then on to the visible light spectrum, then to infra-red and finally radio waves or hertzian. At each level of descent the waves differentiate from each other by frequency, amplitude and polarity. "

"Consider the hertzian level as the slowest vibration, which allows the spin of the atoms to coagulate and bond together in a variety of patterns and arrangements depending on their electrical charges. This is the basis for all chemical reactions and formation of matter. So you can come to understand, my love, that the divine mind and matter are really a continuum of consciousness and energy; from 'no-thing' arises 'some-thing'. All matter is an electromagnetic phenomenon and therefore subjected to the laws of polarity. So what does this actually mean you may ask? Well it means that every constituent of matter has an electrical charge with a value that can be positive or negative. A current or flow is created by the movement of these charges seeking an equilibrium, which either flows away or towards each other. A negative charge is 'attracted' or moves towards a positive charge and alternatively 'repels' a negative charge. This continual search for equilibrium of polarity creates the force that moves your pendulum in a swing of rotation, spin and movement."

"You may now come to understand that you are in effect an electromagnetic being. The very garment that is your body is held together by these polarised particles that are coagulated together to form the molecules and proteins which are the building blocks of your body. Every cell in your body is polarised, right down to those little microtubules I spoke of earlier. Those neuro-chemicals of peptides are polarised, as is the neuronal synapses that fire off impulses of electrical currents in your brain. When I speak of beliefs being like a metaphoric iceberg, then they too are held like little crystallised lattice structures within the neuronal net of your brain's anatomy; they have their own electromagnetic frequency. Your bodily garment and ego itself is a magnetic signature unique to you."

"Now, let's expand on this understanding a little further. The very fact that those magnetic fields, which are attached to the electrical current, are spinning means they are humming or creating a certain tone or pitch. So, once again, if you follow those neat little strings tied off at intervals on your plumb line all the way down you will know them to be a different pitch. At the gamma level the pitch is extremely high, then descending like octaves down each string to finally reach a long, slow vibrational tone at hertzian; which would be like the bass string. Just as your bodily garment is an expression of an electromagnetic frequency, so too does it have a specific frequency and 'pitch'. Therefore, everything emanating from the divine mind down that plumb line is an individuated expression of harmonic sound and electromagnetism."

"Your experience of what you sensually consider as real is confined within this bandwidth of what you are able to perceive. Your eyes can only perceive the visible light spectrum and your ears only a certain pitch; every other level of those descending strings remains invisible and unheard by you in your sliver of reality. This particular bandwidth that you are in effect phase locked in to can be known as your third-dimensional plane of existence. On this plane that is your grand stage of life, you get to experience this feeling of separateness, where there is a duality of polarised opposites and every continuum in between to be experienced. Just as the Divine experiences you as individuated expressions of itself with opposite attributes, so too do you get to experience life as opposite to your true divine nature and essence. The quantum field that you learned about earlier is this duality of waves and particles used to create the visible forms and experiences on your third-dimensional plane of existence that is your grand stage. Everything on this stage will be a reflection like a mirror of your harmonic tone and magnetic signature so you know what your vibrational broadcast is."

"Another feature of your third-dimensional stage of reality, in addition to harmonics and electromagnetism, is symmetry. The very nature of polarity is symmetrical because it is seeking to express the equilibrium of harmony and balance of the positive and negative charges. Symmetry represents the two separated aspects of the whole; everything experienced as duality has this symmetrical feature. This is why I have referred to your third-dimensional stage of reality as being like a hall of mirrors. For all matter there is anti-matter, for every negative electron there is a positron, for every proton there is an anti-proton, every 'spin' has a 'counter spin'; whenever a positive particle is created from the collapse of the wave function, so too is a negative particle created like a shadow. The very wave itself is symmetrical with its undulating crests and troughs. Wherever you see beauty in nature there is symmetry, as it is an expression of balance and harmony. This is often referred to as the 'golden mean' or 'phi ratio', which is a mathematical interpretation of the way nature seems to divide itself up within this rule of proportions seeking balance. You see my love, your grand stage of third dimensional reality is not chaotic and disordered, but rather follows a variety of symmetrical patterns of energy in a constant dance and rhythm of creation. All particles can be transmuted into other particles; they can be created from energy and can vanish into energy. Nothing is permanent and fixed, but always in a constant state of transition and change, moving from one pattern to the next."

"Remember when I said to you previously that seeded within every circumstance is the opposite; where there is adversity there is seeded a blessing, where there is a favourable situation there is seeded a challenge? It can in effect be no other way because of this creative nature and laws that automatically bring into existence the opposite and symmetrical equivalence of every expression of life displayed on your third dimensional stage of reality. When you come to understand *how* your reality is 'constructed' then your relationships and circumstances in your life begin to make more sense. In this context you see that a 'victim' creates the circumstances of its victimisation to mirror back to you this aspect of your ego's personality and judgement. In your relationships you create the mirror of yourself so you can 'play out' these roles as an opposite aspect of yourself. Are you the victim or the victimiser, the rejected or the rejecter, the saviour or the saved, the lover or the loveless, the fearful or the faithful, the prince or the pauper? There are many roles that you have chosen to play."

"You will never remain an enigma to yourself, as all of your circumstances and dramas in your life reveal themselves on your grand stage of life, for the purpose of integrating these separated aspects back into a unified whole of your psyche. The return and unification with the attributes of the Divine always starts with your own inner mental work first with this integration of the separated aspects of your ego. This is why the grand stage of the three-dimensional plane is constructed this way."

"This paradoxical nature of your reality is what the eastern mystics had wonderful understanding of. The yin and yang symbol of the Tao Te Ching is widely used as a symbolic representation of this dynamic relationship between polarised energies; two aspects or opposites contained within the whole. The symbol represents the continuous cycles of change contained within the limits and boundary of the whole, with the two dots representing the ideal that when one of the two forces reaches it extreme, it contains within itself the seed of the opposite. Also, the ancient Chinese text of the *I-Ching* was inscribed with knowledge of the interplay of the polar opposites of yin and yang, which were considered as archetypes to represent all possible cosmic and human situations. The wisdom of the teachings of eastern philosophies is directed at leading a student out of their perceptions of separateness, towards an awareness of a common unity and interconnectedness with the cosmic whole. Duality and opposites are considered manifestations of a basic 'oneness', a dynamic interplay between two extremes, never static, but in a constant dance of transformation and change."

"There was great understanding that the very act of focusing attention on any one concept is to create the opposite. To achieve a balance and harmony of the yin and yang energies through mental disciplines was considered the highest aim of the Sage in spiritual traditions. This is why the practice of meditation is so fundamental to these philosophies; as the silence and stilling of the mind brings the pendulum swing to a place of rest. This is a place of unity and connection with the divine mind itself; for it transcends the ego's judgements that polarise and create the disturbance and suffering in the sentient being's life."

"Now consider this thought if you will. The very wound that you have carved upon your wrist is the sign of a cross. Now this symbol was used in ancient times long before it was adopted by the Christian ethos. Let's now put that symbol in a different context as one being representative of a positive polarity. Imagine each string on your plumb line above the visible light spectrum as a positive polarity and each string below, down to hertzian as a negative polarity. With your new knowledge of the laws of polarity and electromagnetism, you will understand that a negative charge is drawn to a positive charge because there is a field of 'force' that surrounds it and exerts an attraction towards it. Now let's also consider what I mentioned earlier when I said a human entity is created with opposite attributes to that of the Divine; you come to know yourself as a divine being through experiencing the opposite manifestation of your true self, being that of an ego shadow in a physical form. Therefore you are created in a negative polarity or one of 'lack'. It's as if you are a powerful magnet that has been neatly sliced in two, with one pole reaching with a hand outstretched towards the heavens to be reunited with the pole above it."

"You will experience this separation of the two poles as a

yearning and urge to attach, to cling or touch, a constant craving or feeling of discontent; a feeling that you need something else in order to be satisfied. This is the birthing of desires within the human entity that constantly searches for its fulfilment and satisfaction externally to itself. Now add to this the aspect of time in your third-dimensional plane and you have amplified this desire considerably; as all desires have an innate drive to be satisfied immediately. Inner peace seems to be impossible; a state of anguish and impatience is experienced while the desire remains unfulfilled. These unfulfilled desires are what move you around your grand stage of life; for you will always move towards a new situation that you believe will bring you more pleasure and away from something you fear or believe will bring you pain. This force of desire is what motivates every action on your stage of reality."

"I have said to you previously that it is very easy to bring a human entity to the brink of destruction, you take away that which it loves. Further to this truth is to deny an entity the satisfaction of that which the heart desires; this is great suffering indeed. If I say to you that '*satisfaction is the death of desire*', then you would come to understand more clearly that there is great evolutionary advantage in the mental torment and suffering inherent in an unfulfilled desire. For frustrations are what fires the action for change, what moves the entity in search of comfort and peace, to dream the dream of a better day. Evolution is all about change and suffering ignites that purpose; it is what propels a human entity to break free of their ego mould and search for a deeper meaning and purpose in their lives. Remember the caterpillar and the genetic ability of transformation that I spoke of before? An interesting feature of suffering and depression is the physical and emotional withdrawal from society; you stop being your habitual self as the roles you have played have broken down. This solitude allows the human entity an opportunity to develop new perspectives and a deeper understanding about just not themselves but about the world around them. Creativity is an inherent feature of the evolutionary process, because new patterns of organisation and behaviour arise from the chaos of the old. Self-realisation and a rise to higher human potentials emerge as new possibilities in this transition and transformation. Many of your greatest human Masters bear testament to this claim, such as Winston Churchill, Abraham Lincoln, George Washington, Mark Twain, Isaac Newton, Charles Darwin, Emily Dickinson and Michelangelo. All experienced the despair of depression and suffering, yet birthed themselves anew to become creative leaders of their relevant domains. Many a social dilemma has been resolved from insights and revelations arising from the creative mind in a state of turmoil and anguish that has turned inwards to deeper contemplation."

"I know what I talk of may indeed be confronting for you, my love, to perceive your life from an evolutionary perspective rather than the ego self. But I said I would take you to this loftier vantage point of the mountain view so you could understand the hidden forces that rumble down to impact your reality. You are a spiritual being having a human experience, this is a great truth. The desires of your ego are used to this end and purpose; to lead you along a path of self-discovery and realisation towards a remembrance of your true divine nature. All of the laws to what I speak of are designed to create this grand stage of reality you call life; to play your roles and attract the people, events and circumstances that lead you to this divine revelation. Freedom from the manacles of ignorance allows you then to become a lucid co-creator with the Infinite Intelligence of the Divine Creator; to use the laws of creation that I speak of to your advantage, rather than be lost in a valley of perpetual suffering. When I told you earlier, my love, to trust that a blessing will one day come to you, arising like the Phoenix from the ashes of your adversities, then know the law of polarity proclaims this truth indeed."

"Now, to bring this particular teaching home to you and cement your understanding, I want to share some beauteous words inscribed on the *Emerald Tablets* that were found within the Great Pyramids of Giza themselves. They were inscribed by the ancient Egyptian Priest-King Thoth and proclaim:

Aye, know we that of all,
nothing else matters excepting the growth
we can gain with our Soul.
Know we the flesh is fleeting.
The things men count great are nothing to us.
The things we seek are not of the body but
are only the perfect state of the Soul.
When ye as men can learn that nothing but
progress of the Soul can count in the end,
then truly ye are free from all bondage,
free to work in harmony of Law "

The prophet again paused and watched Lilly, looking for acknowledgement of her understanding. With this pause, Lilly asked, "You know this may sound crazy, but what you are speaking of reminds me of all the fairy tales that I read as a child and what I used to read to my son. Every story seemed to have a quest, an overcoming of an adversity of some kind; but every story finished with an ending of 'they lived happily ever after'. So then tell me, prophet, to work in harmony with the laws you have shared and use them to my advantage as you say, how do I do that? Because heaven knows I need my 'happy ever after', I need a reason to keep going because I am so tired of living. So help me understand once again, how do I do that?"

The prophet replied with deep empathy and love evident in his voice, "Indeed, my love, your journey has been a difficult one; but let me assure you the Kingdom that awaits your arrival is a glorious one and well worth your quest. Now, since you referred to a fairy tale, I shall continue with this analogy to assist in your understanding. Let's imagine the plumb line that I spoke about earlier as the tower of a grand castle, with a turret at the top. Inside the tower is a staircase that leads to the top, but there are seven levels, each barred from the other by a locked door. At the top of the tower is a grand book called the 'Book of Life' and it is filled with infinite wisdom. Next to the book rests a pot of gold coins, a treasure indeed for the taking. Now for the soul, its quest is to procure the book and claim its wisdom. For you, however, as a mortal entity standing at the base, you have no interest in wisdom and instead are busy guarding yourself from dragons and demons. In fact, such is your fear that you have encased yourself in a suit of silver armour for protection. This armour is really your ego, bound up in all of its beliefs and attitudes. This armour has a spinning electromagnetic field of force emitting a specific tone and frequency. Now the soul is unable to move by itself as it is locked within your mortal body and armour, so the quest for wisdom must be achieved in unison with you as the mortal."

"The soul now has to fire off a desire in you to motivate you to take the arduous journey up the stairs of the tower. The armour you wear is heavy and cumbersome, which makes the journey a slow and difficult one. In fact the, soul knows that you are unable to complete this journey to the top as long as you are wearing this armour of ego fear. So it fires in you a lofty thought; that there is a treasure of gold hidden within the turret at the top of the tower. This desire for the gold then gets you moving to reach the first step. The soul knows that for the key to be turned is to get you, the mortal, at the same magnetic frequency and tone of that which matches it. Now, knowledge is fundamental to wisdom, because new knowledge creates new neuronets within the mortal entity's brain anatomy, which is generating the electromagnetic frequency and tone. To change this frequency, the mind of the mortal must be changed first and new knowledge is used to this end. As the mortal starts to learn, it becomes aware that it is safe to remove at least the leg armour; which it does so. This small change in magnetic frequency, by changing an inner crystallised belief, now opens the door and the entity steps through to the next level, with a little less armour of fear and a small change in attitude."

"Like breadcrumbs, there are a few gold coins waiting on the step to keep you motivated to continue. Once again, as at every step, new knowledge is used to generate a new neuronal network of electromagnetic frequency and tone that rises to the same level that will match and turn the key of the next room. The higher you go, the more a change in attitude and beliefs are required and the more armour of fear needs to be removed. As the desire grows stronger, you are also polarising the door shut, which adds to your frustration. The greater the prize desired, the more change is required and the more knowledge is needed to rebuild your neuronal network to create a new magnetic frequency. You, as a mortal entity, must become aligned and integrated with the frequency that is your soul, as working in unity is more powerful. This is where the human journey of action moves towards the spiritual journey."

"So, now you find yourself at the highest level, with only one door separating you from your treasure. What would you look like at this level? Firstly, your armour of fear is minimal; maybe just the chest piece is left. On each step of your journey you have been sent various quests and challenges to reveal and overcome your fears. Little by little, each piece of the armour has been gradually removed as your ego feels safer. You have expanded your understanding by new knowledge. Your soul has sent you teachers, books, hierophants and information, leading you towards a remembrance of what you had forgotten of your true divine nature. This expansion of your understanding has changed the physical neuronal network of your brain's anatomy." "You think and behave differently, your reactions and responses are no longer habitual and automatic as they were before. Your attitude is different because your beliefs have changed; you no longer play the victim or martyr because you have a greater understanding of yourself. You are not the same person who started out on this journey. All those changes are reflected as your new magnetic frequency and vibration. The weight of the armour of fear has been shed, which allows your true divine essence to be expressed as a higher vibrational broadcast. What started as a physical journey of endurance was replaced by a mental mastery; you literally changed your mind."

"So what is holding you back from that final door and access to your pot of gold coins you may ask? Now, pay attention my love, for this is the great secret of manifestation and a revelation of your 'happy ever after'. This is where polarity has its greatest influence. A desire is a negative polarity sine it is an expression of lack; you are in acceptance that you do not have that which you desire. Every time your ego makes a judgement it polarises and sets the pendulum swing in motion, thus creating the symmetry of the opposite that I spoke about earlier. So how do you open the door if it is polarised shut? You change your polarity, you start with the opposite. All of the mind work that you have done to get to this final door has been doing just that. Fear is a negative polarity, as is a victim, so too is every negative belief, attitude and emotion that was polarised to attract its opposite. Everything that is a negative polarity is an indication that you are out of vibration and tune with your divine essence; you are a polarised opposite and a distortion waiting to be united and tuned into the divine mind. It means metaphorically the turret is still above you; there is still work to be done."

"Every time you changed a belief, an attitude, an emotion of fear, you changed the polarity. Now the ultimate aim is to stop the pendulum swing all together. This is to release your ego's judgements that polarise the door shut. When the pendulum rests, it is in alignment with the divine mind and the key is turned. So how do you stop the pendulum? You see the pot of gold on the other side of the door in the same mind as the Divine; this is the 'at-one-ment' I spoke of earlier. You close your eyes to the sensual reality and go within; you use your imagination. What is it you believe that a pot of gold will bring to you, why do you desire what you do? You will find this answer will always come back to a feeling. You want to feel at peace, abundant and prosperous, loved, secure, significant, valued and you want to experience contentment and fulfilment. Once you know what feeling you are ultimately desiring, then start with that end in mind. In the divine mind there is no separation; everything is abundant, peaceful, loving. It is whole and complete unto itself; it is the absence of any desire, need or want. This is the state of being you match; you become its equivalence, a perfect state of harmony and balance."

"Now, you may ask, how will the Divine know that I want that pot of gold if I don't ask for it? The divine mind already knows what you want and desire, because all your mortal life you have been firing off those rockets of desire with every event and circumstance that has come into your life. That is what has brought you to this point at the final door of the tower. Your imagination and dreams *are* the divine mind. The Divine has been waiting for you come and get it to come to a point of realisation that you are a powerful divine creator and to free yourself from the armour of fear and weight of limitations. Once you have released yourself from all that load you will fly, you are free and that door opens because you are seeing everything in the light of the divine mind. You are then a vibrational equivalent, a magnetic frequency, a new tune that is at one and unified with the Divine itself. All those stairs and rooms with their keys have led you home; the soul to its wisdom and you to your desires."

"Every one of those rooms and keys are a training ground for mental mastery. You come to learn what you think matters. The universe is consciousness and energy; that is what creates your reality. Your thoughts are a powerful, vibrational broadcast extending far beyond the limits of your bodily flesh. They are the creative force of the universe."

"Now, with this understanding in mind, and your new knowledge of some of the laws of creation, let's again return to an image from your past from the perspective of an observer. Keep in the forefront of your mind that you are surrounded with a powerful vortex of spinning, oscillating energy that emits a vibrational frequency out into the ether and returns. All of your experiences will be in accordance with this law of attraction."

"So once again, my love, just watch ....just watch."

CHAPTER 12

New York
July 2005

As Lilly closed the door of the taxi cab, she stood for a moment on the pavement; a rush of people walked past her, their eyes focused ahead with intent and purpose. She looked towards the hotel and then upwards at the floors rising skywards. Pulling the crumpled paper from her jeans pocket, Lilly again read the note that had been left on her work desk.

> Hi Lilly.
> A guy named Mitch called today
> and asked me to give you this message.
> Said he would be at the Strand Hotel,
> 33 West 37 Street, Manhattan.
> Room 503 until Thursday.
> Jeb

Her heart had skipped a beat when she had read it for the first time and now it was doing the same all over again. She was nervous but excited at the same time; a million butterflies were loose inside her, fluttering away with their breezy wings.

Well, here goes, Lilly thought to herself, as she approached the glass doors of the hotel, which obediently slid open. She made her way through the foyer and past the reception area, returning a smile to the neatly groomed man behind the desk watching her entrance. Entering the elevator, Lilly pushed the button for the fifth floor and waited patiently as it started to ascend. As the doors slid open she made her way down the carpeted hallway until finally she stood in front of the door with the brass numbers of 503 glistening at her. Sucking in a few deep breaths in an attempt to calm her nerves, Lilly knocked on the door and waited.

As the door opened Mitch Andaman stood there; blue jeans and black polo shirt hugging the muscular body she had remembered and so deliciously devoured at their last meeting. His face burst forth into a smile and Lilly felt her knees go to jelly.

"Hey, Lilly, you made it, fantastic. I didn't know if you would come or not. Come on in," Mitch said enthusiastically, as he opened the door wider for her to enter.

"I got your message. Of course I would come and see you again. I'm glad you let me know you were here," Lilly said as she entered the room and placed her brown leather overnight bag on the bed.

Turning to face Mitch, she watched as he moved towards her and wrapped his arms around her, embracing her in a warm hug. She could feel the warmth of his body flood through her, sending an electrical spark tingling through her. Lilly thought she could have stayed there forever; never let him go again. As she was lost in that moment, Mitch said, "It's so good to see you again, I'm glad you came."

Finally pulling apart, Mitch stood in front of her, holding her hands in his.

Lilly looked into his beautiful brown eyes that had locked into her own and said,
"When you left that day I honestly thought I would never see you again. But here you are! It's hard to believe you're standing here in front of me. It's like a dream."

Mitch replied, "Well, I've never stopped thinking about you, about that day we spent together. So I'm not a dream. I'm all yours, Lilly."

"So how come you're in New York? Are you going back to Afghanistan?" Lilly asked him; hoping in her heart that he would say that he had come all this way just to see her.

"Yep, I'm on my way back for another tour. I wanted to see you again before I left," Mitch replied.

Lilly pulled away and turned towards the window to look outside, considering what he had said, not sure how to tell him. "This is really nice. You have a great view of the Empire State Building," she finally said. "I love New York. It's so alive."

Mitch stood behind her and placed his arms around her again, resting his face against her hair. As his hand ran softly across her midriff, Lilly froze and thoughts raced through her mind. She pulled away and turned to face him again, saying, "Mitch, there's something I need to tell you."

Mitch stared back into her eyes, curious at what Lilly was going to say. "Sure, what is it?" he replied.

Lilly's mind was racing; *just say it, spit it out, just tell him!* Finally, after some hesitation, she said, "Mitch, I'm pregnant."

Mitch stood there, stunned, not quite sure he had heard correctly. His eyes fell to her stomach, but the loose shirt hid any hint at what lay beneath. Finally, he said, "You're pregnant?"

"Yes, I'm pregnant. It's our baby, Mitch. You're the father," Lilly replied.

Pulling away from her, Mitch held the look of utter confusion, his mind exploding with the bombshell of revelation that Lilly had fired upon him. He then asked, "How far along are you?"

Lilly replied cautiously, "Four months, I'm due in late December."

Mitch turned away, running his hands through his hair, confusion racing through his mind. "Are you sure it's mine?" he finally said, turning to face Lilly.

"Of course I'm sure, you're the only one I've been with for a long time. You're the only one I've ever felt this way about. I loved you, Mitch, I still do," Lilly replied tenderly.

With absolute frustration evident in his voice, Mitch asked, "Why didn't you terminate it? I live in Australia, for heaven's sake. I'm a soldier, you must realise I can't be here for you?"

His words stung her, cut into her heart and pierced it. "I'm a Catholic, Mitch.I couldn't terminate, I just can't do that," she replied.

"Well, that didn't stop you from sleeping with me, did it?" Mitch replied quickly, looking at her intensely.

Lilly reeled as his words cut deeper into her heart, penetrating to the core. She was silent, just looking at him, her mind struggling with what to say. Finally she said, "I fell in love, Mitch. I didn't just sleep with you; I loved you. I didn't think I was ever going to see you again, so this baby is special to me, it is a part of you that I get to keep. I don't expect anything of you. That's why I never contacted you in Perth to tell you. I don't expect anything. You are free to walk away. We'll be OK without you."

"Lilly you're only twenty-two. You have your whole life ahead of you. You were going to be a teacher, now I've come along and stuffed up everything. What were you thinking? *Damn!*" Mitch replied, pacing back and forwards as Lilly stood there like an innocent child in the principal's office.

Lilly walked towards the bed and sat down, not sure if her legs could hold her any longer; then said, "I'm not a child, Mitch and you didn't stuff anything up. The way I see it is that two beautiful, special people in our lives died; that's what brought us together. I think that maybe there is a reason that things happen, that God meant for us to meet. The chance of me getting pregnant is so remote, yet that's what happened. Maybe something beautiful has come from the heartache and loss we've both experienced. A baby is a new life coming into the world and I want to be a part of that, with or without you."

As Mitch looked at her, he felt Lilly as a stranger, that he didn't really know this woman sitting there. "Lilly there is no reason for anything. That is just some fantasy trying to make sense of Sophia's death. I live in the real world. I don't get to see some God on the battlefield with death all around me. People die, that's just the way it is. They don't die for any reason, there is no grand plan that some so-called God resides over; that's just fantasy."

Lilly raised herself off the bed, grabbed her bag and started walking towards the door, "Maybe I should go," she said, "this isn't really going anywhere and we are just hurting each other and I don't want to do that."

"*Wait! wait!* Please don't go yet. I didn't mean to offend you. I'm sorry if I did that. I'm sorry. I'm just in shock, that's all. I wasn't expecting this and I'm just not sure what to do or say. So please, just stay so we can work through this, hey? Please?"

Lilly paused for a moment then turned and looked at him. He was so beautiful, despite what he had said; she could feel his loving heart that she had connected with the very first time they had met. There was something special that kept pulling them back together.

She placed her bag on the floor and returned to sit on the bed, not sure what to say any more.

Mitch sat down next to her and after a moment of silence said, "I'm not sure what to do. I'm responsible for this and I just don't know what to do. I'm going to Afghanistan, anything can happen. I may not come back, Lilly. That's the truth of it. I have nothing to offer you. I live day to day because that's how I've learned to get through the job that I do. That's how I survive."

Lilly felt a chill run through her body. She knew he was right; he was a soldier. He lived in a world that she had no concept of; she had no idea of what he had experienced and seen. Finally she said, "Well, at least you know. You could have gone your whole life never knowing, so at least now you know. Maybe it gives you something worth living for, to keep you going, a reason to come back. I don't know. You decide in your heart what you want to do with all this. To me this baby is a beautiful gift, a sign of something very special between us. That's how I choose to see it."

Mitch sighed heavily and rubbed his hands over his face. Eventually he stood and went to the window looking out over the view of New York before him. After a moment he turned to Lilly and said, "Look, maybe we could get some fresh air and walk for a bit, get out of this hotel room. We could get a bite to eat and a drink, just relax and talk about this, hey? Would you like to do that?" Mitch asked.

Lilly stood and replied, "All right, that's a good idea, fresh air would be nice."

Mitch grabbed his wallet and keys lying on the bedside table and moved towards the door. As he locked the door behind them they made their way down the hallway to the elevator. After the short ride to the ground floor foyer and out onto the pavement of West

37th Street, where they began walking. When they reached Sixth Ave, Lilly said, "If we go this way it ends up at Central park, have you seen Central Park before?"

"No I haven't. I've only been as far as the airport and the hotel," Mitch replied, taking hold of her hand as they walked. "Have you told your parents yet?" he asked.

"No, I haven't told anyone yet. They are Catholics, so I'm not sure what their reaction will be. But I'll tell them soon and then see what happens; *'fire and brimstones'* for me," Lilly replied with a hint of laughter in her voice.

"I'm sure they'll understand. You are beautiful you know and I appreciate you telling me about the baby, I really do," Mitch replied, squeezing her hand a little tighter, then asking again, "So what about college, how are you going to do that and raise a child? Have you thought about that yet?"

Lilly shrugged, "I'm still getting used to this all. I'm not sure yet. It will work itself out. You don't have to worry about me, you know, I'll be OK. Like you said once before to me, *'just keeping moving on with my life'*, well that's what I intend to do, Mitch."

"Yea, well aren't I the master of advice, the king of walking away from people, that's me," Mitch replied.

With both lost in their own thoughts, they walked on in silence, until Mitch said, "There's a Starbucks, shall we get a coffee?"

"Sure," Lilly responded, grateful the silence between them was broken.

As Mitch opened the door Lilly entered the café and approached the counter. There were a few people sitting comfortably at tables, drinking their coffees and chatting. The young Asian male behind the counter stood smiling, ready to take their orders.

Turning to look at Mitch, Lilly said, "My shout, what would you like?"

"OK, just a long black would be great, thanks," Mitch replied.

Lilly turned to the Asian man and said, "A latte and a long black, thanks."

"I'll just grab some sugars," Mitch said as he walked over to the service counter.

As Mitch reached the service counter, the sound of people screaming made him turn; his heart-beat going into overdrive as he did so. The people that had been sitting were running out the door, while the three people behind the counter were standing, frozen, with their arms up. Mitch's mind was racing with a million thoughts, trying to make sense of the scene in front of him. In a second his eyes focused on Lilly, who had a man standing behind her, holding an arm firmly locked around her neck, his body pushing firmly into the back of hers.

'*Fuck, what's going on?*' Mitch thought with confusion as he moved towards Lilly.

Mitch heard the man scream at the Asian standing behind the counter, "*Just give me the fucking money….empty the till asshole….fucking move…or I'll blow her fucking head off*'

A torrent of understanding flooded into Mitch's racing mind and the adrenalin pumping into his body went into overdrive. He felt his heart thumping inside his chest as if it was going to explode.

Moving slowly towards the man at the counter, Mitch said firmly, "Mate, just take it easy… no-one has to get hurt … just let the lady go …. take your money and go".

As Mitch spoke, the man turned to face him, turning Lilly's body with him. The look of terror in Lilly's eyes drilled into his own as he now saw the gun being pressed firmly into the side of her head. An arm was held tightly around her throat, making her breathing laboured. Mitch's eyes moved to take in the look of the face pressed firmly against the side of Lilly's. He was young and pale, with stubble on his chin and hollow cheeks; a grey hoody covered his head. His black eyes stared intently back at Mitch; a crazed look that held no fear, a look that seemed to be enjoying the power his weapon was exerting on those around him.

 With his attention now focused on Mitch, the young man spoke with anger at him, "*Just fucking stay back asshole… this has nothing to do with you…. Stay where you are or I'm going to put a bullet through her fucking head and yours.*"

Mitch was in turmoil. He wanted to take this guy out and pound him into a pulp of meaty flesh for threatening the life of Lilly and his baby. He knew he could, this is what he was trained to do. But all he could think of was losing them both. If something went wrong he could lose them both…. and that thought ….. the thought of losing them in that moment became intolerable.

Mitch spoke again, slowly but firmly, "Look, you're hurting her…..just let her go…that's all you have to do…just let her go."

With an obvious enjoyment of the confrontation, the guy smiled insanely at Mitch and taunted, "*You want to be a hero, huh fuckwit?.. Is this your bitch?.. Huh?..
 Is this your little lady? Well come on then… be the hero…come on dude ….show your bitch what happens to heroes…*"

Mitch stared back at him, deep into those crazed, druggie eyes and knew this guy didn't care, didn't care one bit whether he pulled the trigger or not. As he looked at Lilly, she stared back at him with wide eyes of terror; the same look of a small child he remembered in Afghanistan. His jaw went tight and his hands clenched into a fist.

Not wanting to provoke the situation, Mitch slowly spoke again, "I'm not a hero, mate… just take your money and go…. let her go…. there's no need for anyone to get hurt… just let her go."

With a repulsive grin showing brown, rotted teeth still on his face, the guy laughed in obvious satisfaction and said, "*Oooh! We have a pussy …. so this is your man bitch ….. a real pussy …..you get to see your fucking hero is really a coward….. maybe I'll just take you with me, huh? … You can be with a real man…. See what it's like to be with a real man, huh?….Wouldn't you love to do that, huh? Maybe we should do that….*"

With anger burning up inside him, Mitch took a step forward and said, "You're not taking her fucking anywhere, scumbag …. Just let her go like I'm telling you."

With the increased threat of Mitch moving towards him the guy moved back with Lilly and then pointed the gun directly at Mitch, "*Stay back fuckwit, come any closer and I'll shoot your fucking head off…..then your little lady can clean up your brains off the floor… she would love that, wouldn't you, bitch?…. would love to do that?*"

Mitch stood there, his eyes locked on to those staring back at him, taunting him, daring him to make another move. The guy was playing him like a game, wanting him to give any excuse to pull the trigger. He looked at Lilly, her brown eyes staring back at

154

him, pleading inside for him not to move, not to do anything crazy. Mitch then looked into the muzzle of the gun pointing at him; he had never been this close to his enemy before. So he stayed still, perfectly still; as long as the gun was pointing at him he knew Lilly was safe. They stood there, in some sort of standoff for what felt like eternity, until the sounds of sirens outside became louder and louder, getting closer.

The police sirens seemed to break through the guy's trance as he turned to the counter and grabbed the pile of bills lying there. As he gave Lilly an almighty shove in the back, which sent her sprawling onto the floor, he yelled, "*Fuck you! You lose!*" He then rammed the door wide open and disappeared out onto the busy street.

With relief flooding through his body, Mitch leant down to Lilly who was lying on the floor sobbing. "Come on, Lilly, he's gone now, it's OK, you're safe now, sweetheart."

He helped her to her feet and then held her trembling body in his arms as Lilly cried into his chest, saying, "I thought he was going to kill us both, Mitch, I was so scared."

Mitch stroked the back of her hair and continued to hold her. He had never felt so needed in his life or felt so much love for another person than in that moment.

He said softly, trying to soothe her, "It's OK babe. We're all safe, that's all that matters. Now, let's get you out of here."

Putting his arm around her shoulders, he led Lilly outside. The Asian guy was outside talking to two police officers standing next to their police car with lights flashing on the top. He pointed to them both as they emerged from the cafe. The officer moved towards Mitch and Lilly, holstering his gun in the process.

"Are you two OK? Is anyone hurt?" the police officer asked with concern as he gently touched Lilly on the arm.

Mitch replied, "Yeah, we're OK. Just a little shook up."

"Are you able to give me a description? We'll put an APB out on this guy," the officer replied, satisfied that they both seemed to be unhurt.

As Mitch described the gunman, the officer wrote down all the details in his blue notebook, then said, "Great. I'll be in contact so we can get both your statements, but you are free to go. Thanks for your help."

The officer then quickly walked off towards his vehicle. Mitch led a shaking Lilly back up Sixth Avenue, heading back towards the hotel.

On arrival back at the hotel, Mitch found the keys in his jeans pocket and unlocked the door to their room. Leading Lilly inside, he said, "Here, just lie down for a bit and I'll get you some water."

As Lilly lay down on the bed, curling herself up, Mitch grabbed a bottled mineral water from the bar fridge and placed it on the bedside table near to her. He then lay down on the bed next to her, facing her on the pillow and softly stroking her face.

"Pity you can't have a stronger drink, I could get you drunk and take advantage of you all over again, hey?" Mitch said with a laugh in his voice, trying to lighten Lilly's distressed mood.

Lilly managed a smile and said, "That was just crazy, it all happened so fast. I can still smell him. He smelt so revolting…*uhh!*"

"Well, he didn't look too crash-hot either; he was high on something, that's for sure," Mitch replied, before adding, "Do you need to go to the hospital, to check if the baby is OK?"

"No, I think I'm OK. I feel all right, just a little shocked, that's all," Lilly replied.

Mitch looked deep into her eyes and felt an overwhelming love rush throughout him. Something had changed deep inside, he could feel it. Finally he said, "You know, I have never felt like this before in my life. I am so used to seeing so much death around me. I never let myself get close to people just in case they die, just like Ric. I protect myself. But looking at that guy today I see how easy it is to destroy a life. It doesn't take much… just pull a metal trigger. But to create a life… that's big… that takes a lot….to bring a new little person into the world…to raise a child …that takes more ….a lot more."

Lilly watched him talk, listening to him speak from his heart. She took his hand and held it tightly, subtly urging him to continue, to express what he was thinking.

After a moment, Mitch continued, "I love you, Lilly, I realise that now. I love you so much. The thought that I would lose you and the baby today just ripped my heart out. I can't stand that thought, babe."

As Mitch propped himself up on his elbow, he moved closer to Lilly and held his hand gently on the side of her face, saying, "I've decided I'm not going to walk away from the best thing that has happened to me in a long time, I'm not going to do that. If you can wait for me to come back, I'll do Afghanistan for the last time. I'll get a discharge and I'll come back and we'll do this

157

together, hey? Raise this baby together…. So will you marry me babe? Will you marry me?"

Lilly's mind was in turmoil; she couldn't believe what she was hearing. This man that had shown up in her life and had swept her heart away was now asking her to marry him. The tears welled into her eyes, her love for him overwhelming her, as she said, "I love you so much, Mitch. Yes, of course I will. You are going to be an amazing dad…just amazing!"

Lilly moved on to him, swallowing him up in an embrace, letting her kiss be long and tender.

Finally emerging, Lilly looked into Mitch's eyes that were glistening, and said, "There's one more thing I need to tell you."

Mitch flopped backwards onto the bed and flung his arms out to the side and said jokingly, "*My God*, you are a lady of mystery aren't you? Full of surprises….Go ahead, tell me…I'm sure there's nothing left that can blow me away today. What is it?"

With Lilly leaning on to his chest and looking him in the eyes, a wide grin settling upon her face, she said, "The baby is a boy."

CHAPTER 13

As the scene before Lilly slowly faded from view and the holographic illumination of the prophet again returned, the dam of grief within her burst forth and Lilly broke into intense sobbing.

The prophet, watching her with overwhelming warmth and compassion, quietly said, "Just let it out, my love …. Just let it go …. Just let it all go."

After a few moments, Lilly looked at the prophet through tear-filled eyes and pleaded, "*Please stop.* I can't do this anymore, *please!* You are hurting me. You aren't human, you don't feel suffering. You are full of these philosophical and scientific explanations, but you don't understand how I feel ..... *it hurts.* My heart is aching so much. I was so happy and now I've lost *everything!* You don't know how many times I look back on that day at the coffee shop and wished that man had just pulled the trigger, to have ended it all then…. on that day. I would have never known this heartache of loss that I have right now… I would have never have known that.
So please let me go…. I want to die …. just let me go… please!"

As the prophet waited silently for Lilly's distress to ease, he finally said, "I do understand about human suffering, my love, for I too have experienced many times the life of a human entity with all the losses and heartaches that sojourn endures. I have fought in wars, borne the body of a cripple, lost a child, been riddled with disease, endured famine and starvation and died a violent death tenfold. Yet it has been those very experiences that propelled me in discovery of my own divinity; to purify, life after life, cycle after cycle, plane after plane, every tendency and hindrance that veiled the true glory of the Divine."

"I have lived in times where the revelation of this divinity within was considered heresy and treason, a blasphemy against the ideologies and religious teachings of the times. All of the secrets of creation held by the mystics and sages of ancient wisdom had to be concealed within symbology, alchemy, allegory and parable to be passed on through initiations, ceremonies and rituals of the secret societies. This is the knowledge I share with you. This is why I am here, why I have come back; to be of service to you and lead you back to the light of understanding that has been concealed from mankind for centuries. This is the highest calling of the Spirit, to assist those who have 'fallen' to rise again and remember the forgotten power of their own divinity."

"You call out for death, my love, as you believe it will bring an end to your torment and suffering. You yearn to be reunited with your God, who you so boldly declare has abandoned you in your greatest hour of need. I have laboured long and arduously with you, to slowly lead you to an understanding that you are not separate and isolated from your God as you believe; you *are* a divine being, you *are* the waters of divinity itself, you *are* the fire and spark of life, you *are* the creator and the created, this is your truth to remember and claim. This is your inheritance and birth-right from the day you were born and is now being delivered upon you."

With anger now in her voice, Lilly replied, "Then what sort of Divine creates from a place of suffering and torment? You tell me I am a vibrational energy that attracts what I fear. You tell me I exist in a reality that is polarised to create duality and experience the opposite polarities in my life. What Divine holds itself above and creates a human to the point of frustration by denying what the heart desires? Does the Divine look down on us and expect some sort of devotion and worship from the emotional cripples below? Does it get some sort of warped, sadistic pleasure from this insane creation? If the Divine is so powerful, whole and perfect, then why can't I be that as well? Why can't *I* have the same peace in my human life as well? *Tell me that, Prophet!"*

Considering for a moment what Lilly had said, the prophet then replied, "Once again, my love, your ego projects a judgement that the Divine has some sort of human qualities that acts as an arbitrator to human behaviour, sitting *above* oneself on a throne of privilege, dispensing condemnation or approval to menials below. If this perspective provides you relief and comfort in your times of distress and suffering, then keep it. There is always a choice as to any meaning or attitude you give to a circumstance in your life. However, if your choices of perspective are limited and drive your behaviour towards one of destruction, then new knowledge is needed to provide a more empowering and constructive perspective. This is what I have been endeavouring to do with you, to lead you towards new contemplations and meanings that have been previously unknown to you. A change of even one belief can propel your behaviour and life in a totally new direction. So let me continue to expand your understanding with this end in mind; to find those new meanings that serve and uplift you rather than destroy and condemn."

"When dealing with beliefs and meanings, let us start with the 'mother lobe', that sponsoring thought that lies behind the mortal entity's motivations and actions; as thought is the ancestor of action. That belief is, 'I die'. With your understanding that the first law of the divine is 'I exist' and the third plane of existence upon which you dwell and experience is created with polarity and hence duality; then this belief of
'I die' is an expression of the exact opposite aspect of the Divine's will, that of
'I exist'. The belief that you, as a human mortal existing within the boundaries of flesh and blood, will *die*, generates every fear held within your brain's anatomy. To the average human entity, death is considered a catastrophic crisis, an abrupt ending and

conclusion to all plans and projects; the absolute cessation of all that is desired, familiar and loved. The plunge into uncertainty and the unknown is entered by the ego who considers its own demise as the complete finality and negation of all aspirations, intentions, thoughts and desires held at the central core of its being. You will see that when your ego holds this perspective and meaning of death as its foundation, then the loss of your loved ones, through death or abandonment, generates the secondary thought of, 'I can't live without you'. This then propels your suffering and distress towards the state of mind that suicide is the *only* option for alleviating your predicament. It may become obvious to a reasoning mind then, that to change your belief and meaning of death will produce a corresponding action and behaviour *away* from contemplation of suicide. So let us see if I can procure that end with you, my love."

"Firstly, let me show you the power of the transformation of words. The word death is held within your mind as an associative memory containing all your beliefs, meanings and definitions compiling a specific neuronal-net of expression. If you had no word of death in your memorised vocabulary, then there would be no neuronal-net and hence no triggering of all the associated memories downloading into your mind of what this word means to you. So with this in mind, let's create a new neuronal-net, free of all such encumbrances and instead call it a 'cycle of rebirth'."

"Now, this cycle of rebirth can be imagined as a great wheel driving 'Involution' and 'Evolution' that I have continuously referred to. Let's go back to the original image of the circle, complete and whole unto itself; the absolute, the supreme creator I call the Divine. Then, again imagine the 'dot' in the centre, as representative of the first breath, the first spark, the first word, the first 'thought' of the Divine expressing the mandate 'I exist'. From this first cause, *all* of the laws of creation came into being in accordance with this mandate and hence 'life' became the *only* expression possible; meaning, it is not possible for the Divine to never *not exist*. So, from this understanding, call forth from your memory the axiom I spoke of earlier, 'As above, so below; so below as above'. If you *are* a divine being as I proclaim, then you too must be *life*, you must *exist,* you can never *not exist*."

"So, lets' expand this concept further. The cornerstone of my teaching is that consciousness and energy create the nature of your reality. There can only ever be *'I'* as the divine mind, a singularity, a non-duality, a non-separation, so consciousness and energy are really synonymous. But to assist you in this understanding I am separating them as individual entities. Let's consider the *'I'* as consciousness; what does that actually mean? You may remember, my love, your experience on the frozen lake where you 'blacked out' and lost what you know as your consciousness, your 'awareness' of your physical sensations and environment. In the same context, consciousness of the divine mind is conscious of itself; it is self-aware, it is thought, it is memory and it learns from feedback, just like you do, in order to grow and expand, to evolve. This is the universal mind, the Akasha, the torsion, the non-local quantum field and most commonly referred to as 'Infinite Intelligence'. Remember what I told you previously, consciousness *is* the 'observer' in the quantum field. This field is holding as a memory all of the 'possibilities' and 'probabilities' of creation. Every thought that has even been and ever will be is recorded within this universal mind of the Divine and is available to *all* life expressions, formed and formless. *Everything* in the universe has consciousness, just in differing degrees."

"Let's now consider energy. *Everything* in the universe is energy. The law of conservation includes the scientific fact that energy can neither be created nor destroyed; it can only change *form*. Equilibrium is a fundamental feature of energy as it seeks harmony and balance. All forms of matter are energy and they are synonymous; your Master Einstein proclaimed this truth in his formula, $E=MC^2$.

As I said to you before, you are an energetic, vibrational being."

"Let's now merge back together consciousness and energy. This can now be considered as the standard of measurement that is the common denominator used throughout all 'scales' of the universe and creation. Every aspect can now be measured as a 'unit' of expression of 'consciousness and energy' as applied to the whole. This is what enables that axiom of 'As above, so below; so below, as above' to operate. I can take this science into the realms of spirituality and now call that combination the 'Spirit'. The Spirit can be considered as every law of creation, creating to the mandate of 'I exist' through consciousness and energy."

"With this understanding, let me now draw you back to the image of the tower with the seven locked rooms ascending up the staircase that I used earlier. Let's remove the treasure of gold and the Book of Wisdom and replace the top of the tower with a vibrant, shining light. You could imagine it now looking more like a lighthouse. Remember previously I spoke of the process of 'involution', which means that the light in the turret, which is the Spirit, is going to slow its vibrations down through each of those seven rooms until it reaches the slowest point at the bottom. This is where matter coagulates together to take a variety of forms, which includes the human entity. You now have a duality where the human entity in a garment of flesh and blood is the lowest manifestation of the Spirit. The journey back up the tower, using the soul and its Book of Wisdom, is the evolutionary process where the human entity is again raised in vibrations up towards the light. The aim is to have the Spirit within a highly conscious human mortal as the highest expression of the Divine. This cycle of involution and evolution is the cycle of rebirth. Each step on the tower is a cycle within itself, moving consciousness and energy to a higher level than the one before.

It could also be considered as each step being one chapter in the soul's Book of Life that I spoke of earlier. This is the stair-step creation known as the 'stairway to heaven'."

"It is essential that you have an understanding of this cyclical nature of your current 'life' as it assists you with changing your perspective and attitude. So I am going to labour this end and provide you with another aspect of the cycle of rebirth that I speak of."

"Contained and recorded within your holy scriptures are the beauteous words as proclaimed to have been spoken to Moses on inquiry as to the name of the Divine. Those words of reply being, "*I am that I am*'. As simple as these words appear, they contain within them the entire understanding of the cycle of creation."

"Firstly, is to take the word '*I*'. This is representative of the complete, whole, perfect state of being that is the Divine."

"Secondly, is to take the words '*I am*'. Now you have the first cause of creation expressing as the Spirit. All of the laws of creation are brought into being to manifest every possible individuation or expression of the divine mind. But remember that there is still only *one* consciousness; that is the *only* substantial reality behind everything."

"Thirdly, there then becomes the 'I am that'. This is the part of creation experiencing itself as the 'created', an individualised aspect of the one consciousness. Consider this as you, my love, in your current life. All of the laws of creation are allowing you to experience your 'life' as a reality with all the beliefs, attitudes and meanings you have projected within your ego. At this point you are amnesic and unaware of your true divine nature; you only know yourself as the labels and identity that the ego has created from its personality and temperament. Whatever you attach '*I am that'* to, the laws bring into your experience. This is the role of your ego. Whatever you decree as your being, you will experience. So when you speak of yourself as, 'I am a victim', 'I am in poverty', 'I am unloved', 'I am alone', 'I am unworthy', 'I am undeserving', then all of the laws of creation deem it to be so, as the laws can operate no other way. It is your ignorance of these laws and amnesic state of not remembering your true divine nature that create the foundations of all your suffering and despair. Your states of being expressed as a 'lack' are creating the reality that is mirroring those 'I am that...' declarations back to you."

"Finally, there is the *'I am that I am'*. This is the integration of those individualised aspects of the Divine back into the awareness of its divinity. As a mortal human entity, you reclaim your knowledge and understanding that you are not your ego, as you believed, but a divine being. Now this awareness for the average thinking man comes through what you have called 'death'; for when the Spirit withdraws the lifeforce of energy and consciousness from the human entity at the end of the cycle, the flesh breaks down and disintegrates its atoms into another expression. But the *essence* of who you are as a light-body or aspect of the Spirit is never lost or destroyed, as you are immortal consciousness and energy, infinite and eternal. When your soul is released from the sepulchre of the physical body it is free and in full remembrance of its divinity."

"The second way this integration back into the awareness of your divinity can come, without the need for the human entity to die, is through an awakening. Now this has to be done very slowly as the ego is a powerful programme that dominates your brain's anatomy. It is like waking you up in the midst of a dream, to become lucid and aware. Such an awakening is associated with many losses for the entity, as this suffering rallies the desire for change and shakes the foundations of its perceived ego identity.

Now, you may call this mechanism for awakening 'sadistic' and 'warped', to use your earlier words, but that is only because of the veil of ignorance that shrouds you from knowledge and awareness of the ultimate plan of the Divine. Your ego has no conscious knowledge of the cycles and laws, yet your subconscious and soul carries within it the whole picture and blueprint of creation. You are like a hologram; you are one aspect of the whole holographic picture, but each part when examined individually carries the whole within it. This is because consciousness and energy pervades all. It is the only substantive reality; it connects all life expressions together in a synchronistic expansion of growth called evolution. So you may now come to understand more fully, my love, that the act of suicide is futile, as you are just moving your consciousness from one plane to another. It is always a case of 'no matter where you go, there you are'. "

"As I have told you previously, you are being woken up in the midst of the dream. You are being given the experience of becoming a conscious and lucid creator within the divine mind. Your soul longs for such an experience. You will come to understand that all of the events in your life have propelled you to this 'fall', this exact moment in time where you arrived within this well and your meeting with me. If you ever come to closely examine your life, my love, you would see time after time, that there is a greater synchronicity behind the scenes of the play that ensured this day would come. Where did the decision come from that ensured your arrival in Phuket with your friend on the day a tsunami would strike? Why was one woman's life cycle ended and yet the life of a boy was saved? How was it that on the other side of the world in Afghanistan on exactly the same day, another event was occurring that would eventually result in a union with your husband? What events evolved from the loss of one soldier's life that day, but ensured the continuance of a little girl's? What events did it take for a man from Australia to arrive

167

at a place in time where his destiny crossed with yours and resulted in the conception of a new life? How was it that your arrival at the coffee shop coincided with a hold-up that propelled a change in your husband's attitude? And why was it that day on the lake you were saved, yet your son was not?"

"You see, synchronicity is the demonstration of the great cycle of rebirth. It is a revelation that there is a greater purpose and reason behind all happenings than you are ever consciously aware of. There are cycles within cycles, but like a wheel they are all connected to the 'hub' of the Divine. Every cycle is an ending and a beginning, just as your scriptures proclaim, '*I am the Alpha and Omega*'. When the human entity attaches and clings to old cycles, this is where suffering and despair arise. Grieving is indeed a natural process and recognition of an ending, but it should also be balanced by an understanding that by letting go and releasing the old, this allows a new cycle to be recognised and embraced. When you consider your son's passing in this perspective, my love, you will come to see that his cycle of life is eternal, his essence of consciousness lives forever more. His passing was not in vain and void of purpose, but instead he has bestowed upon you the greatest gift one soul can ever endear to another, that of an awakening in the midst of life to the awareness of your own divine nature. A grand gift indeed."

The prophet went silent as he patiently watched Lilly, whose eyes were filled with tears that were running gently down her face. Finally, after some moments, Lilly asked, "Then tell me, prophet, what is my purpose? What is the grand plan of the Divine that my son's life was given to awaken me to? Help me understand, please,
so I can find a place in my heart that can let me move on with my life. I need to know my beautiful son's life and passing were the gift that you speak of. Please tell me."

The prophet replied lovingly to Lilly, "Indeed, my love, this I will do.

Now, let your mind once again be filled with the image of the tower with the light shining brightly at the top, like a lighthouse. Remember again the process of involution where the consciousness and energy I called the Spirit is stepped down through each room, which results in the individuation of Spirit expressing into an oversoul, a higher self, a soul, a light-body, an astral body and finally a physical body. You end up being somewhat like a set of nested Russian dolls. By the time your physical body has been birthed you are surrounded by bands of energy and consciousness, which makes you a being with a very specific electromagnetic frequency unique to you. These bands are invisible to you as they are vibrating and spinning at a higher frequency, but they are what connect you like a golden thread to the divine mind and Spirit whilst in a physical body. You are simultaneously an immortal being and a mortal body, the infinite surrounding the finite, the invisible surrounding the visible."

"Let's now add another term which is synonymous with consciousness and energy, that of 'information'. Whenever I speak of consciousness and energy, then information must be included, they cannot be separated, since all energy carries information. Even your science declares this truth, as the quantum physics that I have spoken of is based on quanta sized packets of energy. The mathematical equations used by scientists to understand this phenomenon are making known this information hidden within the microscopic realms of creation. Mathematics is the language of the cosmos. Mathematics reveals that the laws of creation are immutable and unchangeable. Herein lies the ultimate paradox; the immutable laws propel the change that drives evolution. Once you *know* the operation of the laws, then you will know how to consciously create. This is the aim of your awakening, to make you a lucid co-creator; to align your physical body, your soul and your mind with that of the divine mind. You

169

become a clearer vessel, a channel, a receiver of higher vibrations of consciousness, energy and information."

"Now, here is a great truth that has been veiled from your awareness, your brain is a receiver of thought. Your brain does not create consciousness, but is itself *created* from consciousness and energy. When I say you are created as a frequency-specific human entity, then this means your brain has been programmed to only receive a certain frequency band of information. This is the role of your ego identity; it acts as a transducer, a resistor so to speak, limiting the vibrations of unlimited energy and consciousness down into the vessel and form that is your mortal, physical body. The ego limits your receptivity by fear, beliefs and meanings that continually judge and polarise those thoughts into the small, close-minded and doubting personality consistent with your ego's perceived identity. This ignorant, fearful and unknowing state of your ego's personality is your greatest limitation. Now you know why I have endeavoured and laboured this day to bring into your conscious awareness the workings of your ego with all its fears and beliefs, because they distort and reduce your ability to receive the higher realms of thought from the divine mind, from Infinite Intelligence."

"Picture in your mind once again, my love, the image of the pendulum. From the divine mind the plum line represents the descent of the Spirit down through those slowing vibrational levels to you as the solid pendulum. So the Divine fires off a thought down that plum line and it is received by your brain as an electrical impulse. Now some thoughts are so lofty that they are shut down immediately and don't even enter your awareness. Other ideas and thoughts are received and go through the filter of your ego called the recticular activating system and into the neocortex that draws to it all of the associative memories that fit with your own autobiography; that is, the story of your ego self and identity that has been remembered. Now that thought that has been subjected to judgement by your ego filter, is pruned and trimmed to fit with what is familiar and common to your 'story'. This judgement has now polarised the energy of that thought and set in swing the pendulum of polarity and opposites. The modified thought that has now been edited by your ego then returns up that plum line as a broadcast back to the divine mind. This intelligence then receives it, looks for a thought in the quantum field of 'probabilities' and 'possibilities' that matches it and sends it back. This feedback loop could be imagined as a figure 8, a mobius band or a torsion field. It is a constant loop of sending and receiving from your own consciousness back to the divine mind then back to you every billionth of a second, but always coming back modified to fit the feedback from each thought. This is why I have continually referred to you as the co-creator of your reality, because your own consciousness and the divine mind are always connected and in constant communication creating the nature of your reality."

"You need to understand that the universe is a 'mental' phenomenon; there is a fundamental self-aware intelligent force driving all of creation. What you *think* matters. What you *think* creates all of the forms expressing as people, places, things and events appearing to you as your perceived reality. Thoughts are a powerful, creative energy of light. Fear and limiting beliefs are a distortion, a low vibrational frequency put out by your ego."

"Now, remember the image of the pendulum mentioned before that had six strings tied off at neat intervals on the plum line, being representative of the vibrational energy being slowed down. When the light of the Spirit reaches the visible light spectrum it splits; the white light looks like a rainbow prism. This is the creation of the third- dimensional plane of reality with the space-time construct. Your ego, as a personality programmed genetically and through social consciousness, is designed specifically for this plane. The ego, with all its fears and limiting beliefs, provides the blueprint for the soul to experience the feeling of separation and disconnection from the Divine. This is the 'I am that..' part of the cycle of rebirth that is propelling the growth and expansion of evolution into more complex systems. The pendulum, being your ego's personality, does not remember or know that it is *always* connected to the plum line of gold thread to the Spirit, as it is a human entity dependent on sensory stimulation for perceiving what it considers reality. Now your ego's personality, as I told you previously, is polarised in the negative, in one of 'lack', as this creates the pull of desire towards the positive polarity of the Spirit. This creates the love story of life. Seeded within the soul was this safety net, that when the human entity became so lost in this darkness of feeling separated and disconnected it would always be powerfully drawn to reconnect through the energy of love. The feeling of being loved and connecting with another human entity is a remembrance of this eternal connection with the light of the Spirit; love is a very high vibration because it is in synchrony with the Spirit. What the ego separates, the loving heart unites."

"You see, my love, your appearance in this well was always an inevitability. When the external symbols of your son and husband were removed, you turned to unite with the only remaining source of love and connection you have ever known, that of your God. The very same ego that has been the source of your anguish and suffering has also delivered you into the arms of your salvation and divine revelation. So what is your purpose? Well, you are in the midst of that purpose, which is to correct the distortion of the ego, to remember who you really are; a divine being eternally connected to your source energy and infinite intelligence, the creative power of the universe. When you create from the place of ego you can only receive those thoughts that are a vibrational frequency equivalent to that level of your own consciousness. As the fears and limiting beliefs of your ego's personality are dealt with and released, you become more attuned to the sixth sense you have been gifted with from birth, that of intuition. When you become a conscious creator, lucid and aware of your divine connection, then the inspiration and insights flow from the higher mind into your own mind. You become an integrated being, a clearer vessel and channel to draw down into your physical experience the creative 'possibilities' held as potentials within the quantum field. You become like the artist's hand that paints the beauteous portrait, the poet who pens in ink inspiring verse, the maestro's composition of harmonious opera, the philosopher's deepest contemplations revealing unknown insights or the inventor's hand toiling a new idea."

"Every human entity is seeded with an innate desire to create, an inner passion and excitement to express an aspect of themselves, to reveal an inner gift and talent to share with others. Such a desire is the pot of gold held within the turret of the tower. It is used to propel the human entity along the cycle of rebirth from the 'I am that...' towards the 'I am that I am'. Whenever you are feeling excited and passionate about a particular idea or ideal, then you know with certainty you are walking the path of the Divine; you are connected to your spirit. Even the word 'inspired' reveals this connection, as it means *in–spirit*. To enter into the spirit of something is to attach this essence of divine consciousness. All inspiration, insights, revelations and lofty ideas will come *through* you when you are a vibrational equivalent of that thought being sent from the divine mind. Such is the power of new knowledge as it lays the foundations for receivership; it toils the ground for the seed to be planted."

"You are indeed a neophyte of the great work, my love, to 'make known an unknown'. You, and all human entities are vessels and instruments of expression for the divine will to bestow upon all of humanity every creative possibility waiting to be received and manifested, to be given *life*. The decree of the Divine proclaims, '*Go forth and create and bring all things back to me'.*"

173

Once the prophet had paused, Lilly asked with heaviness in her heart, "Everything you have told me so far makes sense. I believe in a soul and a spirit as you have spoken of, I really do; and I know you spoke of me as being like a caterpillar with the capacity to change and transform. But how on earth can I possibly know *every* belief and fear that I have programmed inside me? I am struggling just to find some meaning in my life, let alone getting excited and passionate about some creativity inside me."

The prophet smiled at Lilly and replied, "*Ah*! Yes indeed, yet another wonderful question. Now, in answer to your question let me use the analogy of a game of chess to assist in your understanding. Firstly there is the game board, which can be imagined as the social consciousness. This sets the stage with all the common agreements and rules of your culture and society. So everyone is in agreement, for example, to expectations such as the sky is blue, babies are born, the earth is round, there is time and seasons and so forth. This could be every consideration that is deemed 'normal' or 'real' to all the players. Now there comes 'you' as a player; so let's say in this game you are the queen. So, as I said to you previously, you have chosen the parents that will provide you with a specific genetic disposition, which is then subject to nurturing and further programming by your culture. You, as the queen, now have all of the attributes, personality and texture that ensures you have the behaviour, habits and responses that are required for this particular game."

"When your ego is imagined in this context, like the queen, you can see that your beliefs and fears serve a very important role in the development of the soul. The very limitations and lacks of the human entity are the engines driving evolutionary change. So you are not meant to change every fear and belief, as this is not possible anyway. But instead, this particular chapter that your soul is writing will have a very specific 'theme' that it is following. I have previously described your soul's journey as being likened to an unfoldment. Whatever beliefs and fears are meant to be changed are known by your soul and spirit; and indeed certain events and circumstances will be created in your life to draw them out into your awareness. You need to trust in this process."

"A significant feature of this sublime design of creation is syntony. Lower vibrations are always drawn to higher vibrations to maintain their synchronicity. Your own vibrations are always naturally being drawn to those of your soul and spirit; and as it does so it triggers anything within the human entity that is not attuned to those higher vibrations. These will be any beliefs or fears that you have that need to be released or reprogrammed by new perspectives and meanings. Whatever change you make within your own ego's programme is a change to *everything*. This is because you are the one interconnected consciousness and energy; so every change at every level is a change to *all*."

"For you, my love, your theme, chosen by your soul has been an awakening within the midst of your life. So your ego programme needs to be birthed anew; and this is what I am going to assist you in doing. To do this, all of your new knowledge about the laws of creation will become apparent. As a human entity on the third plane of existence, live in the world of *effects*; the *causes* flow through from the Spirit, which remember is consciousness and energy. So to change the 'effects' is to first change the 'cause'. How do you do that? Meditation. When you go into meditation you are bypassing the ego. The ego's judgement is creating the polarisation of the incoming thoughts; it is the pendulum swing of life. When those judgements are silenced, even just for twenty minutes every morning, you are connecting directly to the divine mind. This is focus; a powerful, directed, single-minded focus of energy directed straight at the Divine so that you become reunited and one. This state of being is to arrive at 'first cause'."

"Next you need to plant a new seed, a new cause. All of the laws of creation will work exactly the same way, except this time you are creating consciously. So what is the new seed you may ask? It is the declaration of *'I am'*. This can be done in two ways. Firstly by a vocal chant of *'OM'*, which is the sound of the first cause. Secondly, if you choose you can attach the new affirmations of the states of being you want to experience; such as, '*I am* divine, *I am* whole, *I am* perfect, *I am* complete, *I am* peace, *I am* fulfilled, *I am* abundant, *I am* love'. You do this every day and every day you are releasing that focused energy of intention into the quantum field. Then, just like any new seed, you allow the law of growth to do what it does best. You allow everything in your life to be recreated in accordance with those mantras; to cast out anything of old that is not attuned to that intention and bring in the new that is. This takes time, but as you hold firm, with patience and persistence, the new seedling will one day appear, just as the law declares."

"You must come to understand, my love, that all of creation comes first from this place of *being*. You must turn within first, close your eyes to every circumstance external to you and use your third eye, the unseen eye that is your focus. Focused energy is the powerful creative force behind all of your manifested human forms, places, events and circumstances on your grand stage of life. It is the science behind the prayer of gratitude, seeing it within long before it ever appears for you to physically experience. Where your focus goes, your energy follows. When your intention is pure and your motives move beyond the ego's self-centred demands of *'my will be done'*, into the realms of giving and sharing that mirrors the divine mind as a being with a focus of *'thy will be done'*, then you know you are on the path of the heart, the path of the Spirit; then this new reality will be projected back to you."

"Now, we have journeyed together deep into the rabbit hole to reveal much to you this day. Our time is nearly at an end, so is there anything I have shared with you that you don't understand?"

Lilly pondered for a moment then replied, "You have shared so much with me, prophet and for that I am eternally grateful. The new knowledge and perspectives you have shared with me, especially in regards to my son's soul journey, have lifted my heart, so I thank you for that. I feel an enormous weight has been shifted from me, that maybe there is a reason, a greater purpose, lying behind the events in my life that I had been unaware of. I am totally exhausted, but I do understand what you have told me."

The prophet then replied, "Wonderful. Now before I go, I would like to avail to you a few suggestions should you decide to continue with your life's journey. Firstly, to understand that meditation is an essential part of creating your day. You need only twenty minutes first thing in the morning when it is quiet and before you commence your daily activities. Secondly, the knowledge I have shared with you should be expanded upon. Allow yourself to receive the right books, which will find their way into your possession. Also, seek out a hierophant or teacher who has knowledge and understanding of the creative process on this third-dimensional plane of reality and the role your ego serves in that process. Thirdly, become very aware of the role your social consciousness has in perpetuating fear into your reality. Wherever you are confronted with ideologies and beliefs that are founded upon fear, then turn away and find your alternative reality; never let those fear-based beliefs of others in your society rule the domain and treasured ground of your own mind. Think for yourself."

"As you travel forth in this cycle of your life, my love, know that you are never alone; you are loved eternally and held within the loving womb of the Divine. Whenever your journey tires or burdens you, always call upon help in loving prayer of gratitude and know that your prayer has been heard and answered before you have even asked. Everything is perfect as it can be no other way, for the ways of the divine are always one of perfection; trust in that promise. Look for the synchronicities in your life, as they are a sign that every event and circumstance has their perfect place and time. Go and live your life with this grand new knowledge of your own divinity, a blessed gift of remembrance that has been delivered forth to you this day. As you heal yourself, you become the light of the world. You share this healing with all, you become like the living lighthouse, shining and sharing your new awakening to lead the way for all who have fallen. This is your grand love story to write."

"As I bid you farewell, know that I am always at your service; call upon me whenever the need arises and I will appear in ways you may never expect. I may be a book you read, a white feather you find, a coin on the ground, a comment by a friend or a rainbow on a cloudy day; all are signs of the Divine. So, goodbye, my love and always remember, I love you very much you know ..... So be it."

As Lilly sat there, the image of the prophet began to gradually fade and with panic in her voice, she called out, *"But wait! How am I going to get out of here?"*

CHAPTER 14

As the smooth, puffy clouds cushioned against the brightest blue sky rushed past, Lilly held her legs firmly against the sides of the white stallion, holding on to the long, flowing mane of hair with all her strength. She could feel the power of the steed rush through her, as each galloping step stretched its muscular frame forwards and upwards. The giant, white, feathered wings extending from the shoulders of the stallion added to its power and speed, propelling it through the heavens and blueness beyond. Lilly could feel it, could finally feel it in her heart like a long-lost friend returning. She was free... so blissfully....so divinely...free.

"Wake up! Lilly, wake up! Wake up!"

Lilly could hear the words like an echo from the abyss, *wake up...wake up.* But she didn't want to; she wanted to stay, she wanted to feel free. *Just let me be free,* she thought, *just let me be free.* As Lilly fought to keep her slumbering flight, an equal force seemed to be pulling her back, forcing her eyes to open. The brightness of the light burst through and she shut them again.

"Lilly ... Lilly .... Wake up!"

Slowly she opened her eyes again, she could hear her name. The lights were so bright. Lilly struggled to see through the blur, see through the fog at an image starting to emerge. Everything was so white... so white... until finally the foggy image became a figure of a man standing close, leaning over her.

"It's OK Lilly, everything is going to be OK," he said gently to her.

Lilly pulled back, frightened. She realised she was lying in a bed.

She looked around trying to make sense of where she was.

"You're in hospital, Lilly. You're safe now, " he said softly.

Lilly looked at him, not recognising him at all. "Who are you?" she asked, the uncertainty of everything confusing her, struggling to make sense of where she was.

"I'm Doctor Williams. You're in Frankfort Hospital. You have concussion, Lilly, so you may be feeling disorientated and a little confused, but that will pass. Do you remember falling in the well?" he asked.

Lilly looked at him, "A well?" she asked.

"Yes, you were found down a well. You were extremely lucky they found you when they did, especially with this freezing weather. You must have a guardian angel, Lilly, because you didn't even have hypothermia. It was quite amazing. Do you remember going out to Empire Bluff at all?"

Lilly struggled to find a memory; everything seemed hazy and foggy, bits and pieces flashing in and out. "I'm not sure," she finally replied.

As the doctor touched her lightly on the shoulder he said, "Lilly, you were found with a rope next to you, can you tell me what you were going to do with it?"

Lilly looked at the doctor. With the mention of the rope her mind finally began to break through the haziness, began to download with vibrant images flashing into her mind ... *a rope ... driving in her car.... walking ... footprints in the snow.....falling.... stone walls ....a man? ....talking to a man?*

Finally, turning her eyes away from the doctor's, she said, "I couldn't do it anymore."

"Maybe we can talk some more about that later; we may need to have another look at the medications you're on. You'll get through this, you know; you have many people that love you and want to help. In fact there is someone outside who would very much like to see you; do you feel up for a visitor?" the doctor asked.

Lilly returned her eyes to his, not sure who he was talking about. "Yes, OK," she replied.

As the doctor turned and left, Lilly lay there, looking out the window and the grey clouds outside. Confusion reigned in her mind; had there really been a man in the well? Was it all just a dream? It seemed so real.

The sound of the door opening made Lilly turn from the window. Mitch was standing there. Lilly's hands went to her face as she burst into intense sobbing, her body racked by an overwhelming feeling of release. *"You came back ... you came back,"* she managed to say.

Mitch moved towards Lilly and wrapped his powerful arms around her, pulling her into his chest and holding her there as she sobbed. As he stroked the back of her hair, he said, *"I'm sorry Lilly... I'm so sorry...* I blamed you for Richie's death and that was unfair. I see that now. Please forgive me. I love you so much."

Lilly clung to him, not wanting to let him go, feeling the beat of his heart against her own. So she stayed there, releasing all of the tears whelming up inside her, letting all of her heartache go, releasing herself from all the pain and suffering she had held inside eating away at the core of her being. Finally, she said. "There is nothing to forgive you for, Mitch; I understand. We both lost our son and neither of us are to blame for that; it was an accident, no-one is to blame for anything."

Finally releasing her from his hold, Mitch wiped the tears from Lilly's eyes and said,
"You know, I came home today and you weren't there. I just felt this coldness run through me; it was like I knew, I just knew. So I got into the car and drove, I went looking for you. I don't know why I went to the Empire Bluff Trail, but that's where I ended up and I saw your car. When I got out, I started running because I saw these footprints left in the snow and then they turned off into the forest. I got so scared, Lilly. I have never been so scared in all my life than at that moment. I thought I was too late, that I had lost you."

Lilly looked into his brown eyes and could feel him; could feel the warmth of their love surrounding and immersing them together. She said quietly, "I didn't know what else to do, Mitch, I was so tired of living with this heartache. To lose Richie and you was too much, it was just too much to bear. *I love you Mitch…. I love you…*"

"Thank heavens you fell down that well, Lill. I know that sounds crazy, but I can't stand the thought of what would have happened if you didn't," Mitch said quietly.

Lilly stroked his face, feeling the familiar touch, then said, "I had this bizarre hallucination. There was a man called the prophet and he spoke to me. He showed me these visions of my past. It was so crazy."

Mitch smiled, "Well, you have concussion, so hallucinations are normal, you'll be OK."

"It seemed so real, though. He even showed me you in Afghanistan with your friend Richard," Lilly replied, looking at Mitch.

"When you have trauma, Lill, the mind plays funny tricks on you. Like you said it was just a hallucination; you are OK. The doctor told me he wants to keep you in overnight, just to make sure everything is all right; but then you can come home. OK?" Mitch asked, squeezing her hand.

"I have such a thumping headache, so I think that's a good idea," Lilly replied.

"Well, I'm going to just sit here with you for a while, then I'll go home and come back tomorrow to pick you up. Everything is going to be OK, Lill. I'm going to take care of you, I promise," Mitch said lovingly.

Lilly kissed him lightly, hugged him close again and laid her head back onto the soft pillow, feeling the tiredness yet again overcoming her.

Mitch smiled, gently touched Lilly's face and said, "I love you".

"I love you too," she replied.

As Lilly lay there, struggling to keep her eyes open, she could feel Mitch's hand holding hers. She squeezed it a little tighter, not really sure anymore of what was real and what was a dream. Finally, Lilly let go, allowing herself to descend into a peaceful sleep with a final thought spinning through her mind..... *maybe it's all just a dream...just a dream.*

The sound of voices aroused Lilly from her sleep. As she opened her eyes and adjusted to the bright lights yet again, she saw Mitch standing near the door talking to the doctor she had seen the day before. On seeing her awaken they both moved towards her bed.

Mitch took hold of her hand and said, "Hey, sweetheart, how are you feeling?"

Lilly smiled back and said, "I'm OK. I'm feeling much better."

As the doctor took the chart from the end of her bed, he said, "All your signs are good Lilly, so you can go home when you feel ready. I would like you to make an appointment with reception to come in next week so I can see how you are going.
I can take out the stitches in your wrist as well."

Lilly looked at the crisp white bandage on her wrist and then replied, "OK, I can do that."

"Thanks for all your help, doc," Mitch said as he shook the Doctor's hand, before he left the room.

"I've brought some clean clothes for you, Lill, so when you're ready we can go home," Mitch said as he placed a bag onto her bed.

As Lilly pulled herself out of bed, her legs felt weak and like jelly; her whole body felt foreign and new, not yet connected to the ground her feet rested upon. She paused for a moment, waiting to download into her body.

Mitch touched her shoulder, "Are you OK? Do you need some help?" he asked.

"Yes, I'm fine, I just need a moment, everything seems so surreal," Lilly replied.

"I'll wait outside and get you discharged. Just come out when you're ready, OK?" Mitch asked.

Lilly watched as Mitch left the room and after a few moments she finally felt able to move. *Just keep moving,* she thought to herself.

As they drove into the driveway of their home, Mitch helped Lilly from the car and unlocked the front door. She walked through the door and went into the living room, feeling like she had stepped back in time. On leaving the day before, Lilly had never expected to be standing in her home ever again; yet here she was. She looked outside; the snow was on the ground, the vast expanse of the lake splayed before her. A chill ran through her body.

Mitch walked up to her and looked out at the view that had Lilly's attention. He wrapped his arm across her shoulders and said, "I'm glad you're home. I'll make us a coffee and we'll talk."

As Mitch returned to the kitchen, Lilly moved towards the stone fireplace that was alive with a vibrant, burning fire emitting its warmth and heat throughout the room. She stood near it, warming herself. She looked at the portrait hanging on the wall above. The sight of her son's smiling face sent a familiar pang of heartache through her. A memory of words spoken to her fired into her mind ….. *Your son Richie is a beauteous soul….his love has never left you, you know'.*

"Here's your coffee," Mitch said, breaking through her trance.

"Thanks," Lilly said as she took the cup from Mitch.

"Come and sit down, there's something I want to talk with you about," Mitch said as he sat down on the couch closest to the fire.

As Lilly sat down next to him, she held the warm cup in her hands and waited for Mitch to speak.

"Lill, this year has been a tough one; and I know my leaving impacted you far more than I could have ever known. But since I left I've had plenty of time to think about things, to try and make sense of everything. I think if we stay here we are locked into the past. Every day we have to drive past the playground and the lake and that's painful just for me, let alone you. You've left Richie's room just the same and that adds to the pain we live with every day. It's time to let go, Lill, we need to let him go; or this is going to keep tearing us apart and I don't want that to happen to us again."

Lilly watched as she listened to Mitch, the tears slowly running down her face.
"What are you suggesting then?" she asked.

"I want to take you home to Perth. We can have a whole new start. Your family doesn't live in Empire anymore, Lill, but in Perth I have my family and we can be part of a bigger family again. You'll have a lot more support than you have being here all by yourself every day when I'm at work. You can write that book that you've always wanted to do. I'll get a job with the police maybe. It will be a whole new start, babe, a new beginning for us."

Lilly looked at him, her mind racing with a million thoughts, until she said, "I'm not sure Mitch, this is where I was born, my whole life has been in Empire. Letting go sounds easier than you are making it out to be. I would have to apply for a visa, we would have to sell the house and furniture; it is a huge change."

"That's exactly why we should do it, because it is a change, a big change. You nearly died yesterday, Lill, which means we need to do something different to ensure that never becomes the only choice you think you ever have again. Change shouldn't scare you; it should excite you, because it means a new door is opening. This is our new door, babe, so what say we step through it together?" Mitch replied, looking expectantly at Lilly.

Lilly sat quietly for a moment, her mind contemplating words that had been spoken to her, revealing a past remembrance: *"trying to open a door that is closed to you .... next to you an open door of new possibilities ... new dreams ... new life ...waiting."*

Finally she said, "Let me think about it, Mitch. I just need to let that idea settle."

Mitch said, "That's all I'm asking you to do, just at least to think about it as a possibility."

"I do know what you mean about letting Richie go; it is something I had been thinking about in the hospital. I realise now that keeping his room the same is just holding on to the past, which is very painful. I know I need to remember that he is still our beautiful, loving boy, regardless of a room full of possessions that really don't mean anything. So I've decided that I'm going to pack away all of the things in his room today; I am going to at least do that today." Lilly replied to Mitch.

"OK, if that's what you would like to do, then we'll do that together. I'll go and grab some boxes from the garage," Mitch said as he lightly touched Lilly's face and then moved from the couch towards the door.

Placing her coffee cup on the table Lilly rose from the couch and made her way down the hallway. She opened the door and entered. The smell of her son was still evident, it always was; it seemed to carry upon it the most memories. Lilly moved to the bookcase and grabbed a handful of books from the shelf, placing them on the bed. As she did so a bright blue album fell from the pile on to the floor. Lilly picked it up and looked at it. She remembered the album well; she had spent a whole day compiling numerous family photos for her son. Together they had often lain on his bed, flicking through the pages, laughing together.

Lilly sat down on the bed and started to turn the pages. The photos took on a familiar story, embedding a loving timeline of their life shared. From his birth, to his first birthday, a new tooth, a hug with Winnie, sandcastles at the beach and a push on his swing. As Lilly neared the end she paused for a moment on a large photo that was a copy of the one hanging above the fireplace. This was her favourite. The Betsie Lighthouse in the background and the three of them gathered near the snowman. She smiled. Just as Lilly was about to turn the page, she paused, her attention drawn to an image standing on the porch of the lighthouse. *That's strange*, she thought, not remembering ever having noticed it before. Looking closer, she saw it was a figure of a man; a man with short, wavy-brown hair and a beard. His clothes were white.
Oh my God! Is that the prophet?

Lilly bounced off the bed and moved quickly back to the living room, carrying the open album with her. Standing in front of the fireplace, she looked closely at the large, framed photo hanging above. Again she saw the same image of the man standing on the porch of the Betsie Lighthouse. *"It's the prophet! It's definitely the prophet!"* Lilly said out loud.

At the realisation that the image was the prophet, Lilly stood stunned. *It was real ...everything was real....it wasn't a hallucination at all ...Oh my God!*

As Lilly stood there, her mind now going into overdrive at this revelation, Mitch came through the door carrying an armful of empty boxes.

"Mitch, come here, I need to show you something," Lilly called to him, waving her hand frantically.

Mitch placed the boxes down on the table and quickly walked over to Lilly.
"What?" he asked inquisitively.

Lilly held open the album for Mitch to see, pointing to the image in the photo. "See this man in the photo, the one standing on the porch, this is the prophet. This is the man that I said spoke to me in the well. Now look at the photo on the wall, *see*, that's him, *that's the prophet!* I wasn't hallucinating at all; it was real, the prophet was real, Mitch!"

Mitch took the album and looked closely at the picture, then up at the framed photo hanging above, saying, "That's really bizarre, I have never noticed him standing there before."

With excitement now growing in her voice, Lilly said, "Like I said, Mitch, he showed me these visions of my past; that day on the lake, being in Phuket with Sophia when the tsunami hit; he showed me when we first met and went out to the lighthouse to deliver the letter to Ben and Laura. Remember I told you that he even showed me a vision of you and Richard in Afghanistan? I watched Richard die, Mitch! I watched you save that little girl and put her on the helicopter ... I saw that."

Mitch stood confused, looking at Lily as she burst forth with her memories of the prophet, then he stopped her and said, *"Hang on! Hang on a minute, Lilly* … Let me think for a moment… I never told you about the girl who was injured…. or how she came with us on the chopper … So I'm confused … how you could know that?"

"Because I saw it, Mitch, the prophet showed me, that's how I know," Lilly replied.

"This is all very strange, Lilly, but I do believe you."

"I understand now, Mitch, it all makes sense. I wasn't meant to die yesterday, I was meant to end up in that well to meet the prophet. Just as you were meant to come back yesterday and then find me out at the Bluff. What are the chances of you going straight there and then following my footprints that led you to the well? Don't you see? Everything has happened for a reason," Lilly pleaded.

With confusion reigning in his mind, Mitch replied, "Then what is the reason then? What did this prophet tell you that was so important to have you plunge into a well and nearly kill yourself?"

"He told me so many things, Mitch, but he didn't tell me what my future is. He did say that one day a blessing would come and to trust in that. So you're right, Mitch, it's time for a new beginning, time to step through the new door. Let's do it, let's move to Perth, start again and see if that is the blessing he spoke of," Lilly replied with excitement rising in her voice.

Mitch laughed and embraced Lilly in a hug, "You already are my blessing babe, we don't have to travel anywhere to find that. I love you right here and now. You are going to have to tell me everything that this prophet told you, though; so lucky for us the flight to Perth will give us plenty of time to talk."

Lilly smiled back and laughed with him in reply, "Maybe I'll just write it all down for you to read in a book."

CHAPTER 15

University of Western Australia,
Perth, Australia.
Ten years on ...

As Mitch pulled the car into the parking space and turned off the engine, he looked at Lilly and said, "Are you nervous?"

Lilly looked at him and said, "Of course I am, my tummy feels like it's doing cartwheels."

"You'll be great, Lill, once you get started it will all just flow. I'm very proud of you, you know," Mitch replied reassuringly, squeezing her hand.

As Lilly leaned over, she kissed him on the cheek and replied, "Well, hopefully you will still think that way after I've finished."

Opening the door, Lilly stepped out of the car. She ran her hands down the sides of her figure-hugging black dress and her fingers moved to the black pearl pendant hanging around her neck. Satisfied that everything was in its rightful place, she moved to the front of the vehicle and stood looking at the University buildings ahead of her, beyond the grassed lawns.

Mitch joined her, holding the hand of a small child by his side. Lilly looked lovingly at their five-year-old daughter, Grace, dressed in a pink summer dress, dotted with red hearts.

"Can I have an ice-cream Mummy?" the little girl asked, looking at Lilly.

"When Mummy's finished here, then we'll go and get an ice-cream, sweetheart. So you need to be a good girl for Daddy, OK?" Lilly replied.

The three of them made their way across the vast lawn and entered through the doors of the grand Winthrop Hall. The place was abuzz with numerous people, some already seated and others milling around talking. Above the stage hung the banner *The Road Ahead: Inspiring Future Leaders*. Lilly felt her stomach churn yet again with nerves.

As they moved towards the desk adorned with numerous name tags, Lilly picked out two of them, bearing Mitch's name and her own. As she handed one to Mitch, she gently pinned her own tag to her chest. Just as she did so, a women, dressed in smart trousers and tailored jacket, moved towards Lilly with an excited smile on her face.

"Hello Lilly, thank you so much for your time today. I'm so excited that you're here," she said, touching Lilly gently on the shoulder.

Lilly smiled back, recognising the Chancellor and replied, "Hello Helen, thank you for inviting me; there certainly are a lot of people here."

"We hold this event every year. There is always a lot of interest, so it's fabulous to have you as one of the speakers. We'll be starting in about twenty minutes, so when you are ready, just take a seat up on the stage and there are a couple of seats reserved at the front for your family," the Chancellor replied.

"Thanks very much, Helen," Lilly smiled as the Chancellor moved away, disappearing into the crowd.

Standing against the wall with Mitch and Grace, Lilly looked at the throng of people, young and old, parents and grandparents, graduates and teachers. As she stood there, lost in awe, a young man walked up and stood next to her.

"Mrs Andaman," he said, looking at her.

Lilly looked at the handsome face with the bluest eyes and sandy-brown hair now standing next to her. "Yes," she replied, unsure of who he was.

"You probably won't remember me, but my name is Zac. We met in Phuket in 2004," he said.

Lilly's mind was racing, *Zac?* she thought to herself, trying to remember through the haze of memories that surrounded the tsunami and the loss of Sophia.

"I was the young boy you saved," he replied, jogging her memory further.

As Lilly looked at him, the image of the Australian boy with sandy-brown hair, wearing red and white boardies and lying exhausted on the staircase, flooded in.
*"Oh my God!...Zac!.... Of course.... Wow!... Look at you,
.....You're all grown up... This is amazing,"* Lilly stammered.

"I saw your photo on the poster advertising this event and I recognised your face and your name. I never really had a chance to say thank you, so here I am. I am alive today thanks to you. So thank you for being brave enough to save my life that day," Zac said, looking into Lilly's eyes.

Lilly couldn't contain herself any longer and embraced Zac in a warm hug. "I can't believe you're standing here, Zac," she replied, overcome with emotion.

As she finally released him, she asked, "So are you a student here?"

"I graduated twelve months ago with a degree in medicine, so I'm a doctor now. What you did for me that day influenced me immensely; I wanted to save some lives too. I always felt that I survived that day for a reason, so I went into medicine to give back that gift of life you gave me," Zac replied proudly.

"That's just amazing Zac. I bet your dad is very proud of you," Lilly replied.

"Yes, he is. He's always been very grateful to you for helping me find him that day."

As Lilly turned towards Mitch she said, "Zac I would like you to meet my husband Mitch and this is our daughter Grace."

Mitch shook Zac's hand warmly, replying, "Nice to meet you, Zac."

As Zac shook his hand, he commented, "You have an amazing wife, Mitch."

"Yes, she's pretty special," Mitch replied, looking lovingly at Lilly.

Looking at Grace, Zac said, "Your little girl looks just like you, Lilly. I'm going to be a dad myself very soon. In fact, my wife is here today as well. I would love you to meet her."

Turning to face the crowd, Zac waved his hand towards a young woman who was standing with another group talking. On seeing his gesture, the woman walked towards them.

"Darling, this is Lilly and Mitch Andaman. Lilly is the woman from Phuket I told you about," Zac said, introducing her.

Lilly looked at the beautiful young woman, clearly pregnant, with long, dark hair and brown eyes. As Lilly held out her hand to shake the woman's, her attention was drawn to the woman's lower left arm, which was missing. "It's very nice to meet you. When are you due?" Lilly asked with curiosity.

"Lovely to finally meet you too, Lilly. I'm due in four weeks, so Zac and I are very excited," she replied, clutching Zac by the arm.

"I'm glad I'm not the only one with an accent here. Which country are you from?" Lilly asked.

"I was born in Afghanistan. I lived in a village called Alia Bad until my family were killed in the war. I was brought out to Australia as a refugee when I was ten years old.
So I consider myself Australian now," she replied.

As the woman spoke the words Alia Bad, Mitch's mind started to fire with a torrent of memories, pulling him back to his distant past. He looked intently at the woman and the missing lower left part of her arm, then into the brownest eyes that seemed to be so familiar; as if he had seen those same eyes somewhere before. Finally, he looked at her name tag, bearing the name Zahera in bold black letters. With that final piece of information falling into place, Mitch's memory projected into his mind an image of a small girl, dishevelled and crying, her left arm a mangled wound, sitting on a dusty floor surrounded by the dead members of her family.

With that tormented image he finally uttered the words, "Korengal Valley."

As Mitch spoke the words, the woman looked at him, not having heard that familiar name for many years.

"Yes, Korengal Valley. Alia Bad is in the Korengal Valley. Have you been to Afghanistan?" she asked Mitch.

Lilly looked at Mitch, whose face had turned ashen. For her too, the name of Korengal Valley had triggered a memory of the image she had seen within the well so many years ago. She could see on his face that Mitch too, had also remembered.

Lilly turned to the woman and said, "Zahera, Mitch served in the military in Afghanistan. He was there in Alia Bad in 2004."

Looking at the woman, with pain etched on his face, Mitch said, "I'm so sorry for what happened to you and your family Zahera. I was the soldier that was there that day. I put you on the helicopter."

Zahera looked at Mitch and could clearly see his angst and sorrow. It was the same look she remembered as a ten-year- old, the same look she remembered seeing in the eyes of the soldier who had tendered her wound. With that thought, Zahera stepped towards Mitch and embraced him, wrapping him in the warmest of hugs.

As she finally stepped back, Zahera took hold of Mitch's hand and looked into his eyes. "There is nothing to be sorry for, Mitch, you saved my life. I am so grateful to you for that. The war in Afghanistan went for another ten years after that day, so you saved me from enormous suffering and torment if I had stayed. You gave me a whole new life. I'm married to a wonderful man and we're about to have a baby. I've been studying for a Master's Degree in Social Work, so I will get to help thousands of refugees

197

just like I was. You were my guardian angel, Mitch, you just didn't know it."

Lilly smiled and gently rubbed Mitch across his back, "The world is smaller than we ever knew."

Before Mitch had a chance to reply, Helen appeared at Lilly's side, emerging from the crowd. "We're about to start now, Lilly, so could you make your way to the stage and your guests be seated."

"Thanks Helen," Lilly replied, before turning back towards Zac. "I need to go now, Zac, but can you give Mitch your phone number as I would love for us all to get together. There is so much more I would like to know."

"Yes, absolutely," Zac replied.

As Lilly started to move off, Mitch said, "Good luck."

Lilly gave him a nervous smile and then moved towards the stairs and up onto the stage, taking her seat next to several other speakers. She watched as Helen took the stage as well and approached the podium.

"Good afternoon everyone. I would like to thank you all very much for your time in attending this wonderful event today. *The Road Ahead* is an event that has been run by the University for several years now with great success. It has always provided a wonderful opportunity to bring together, as a forum, speakers who share their own wisdom and knowledge with fresh minds ready to embark on their own journey on 'the road ahead'. Our audience tonight includes not only new graduates, but also teachers of the faculty, parents and friends, professions such as doctors, psychologists and social workers; all coming together with a common intention and purpose to provide inspiring leadership towards a service to humanity. This University prides itself on being at the leading edge of bringing together powerful minds to share new knowledge and perspectives in achieving that intention and common desire."

"With that goal in mind, I am delighted to introduce as our first speaker, a woman who dared to share her own story of tragedy and triumph in an international best-selling book titled, *The Well*. This *New York Times* bestseller is now published in sixteen languages across the globe and went on to become an inspiring book of hope and inspiration to millions of people living with depression and suicidal behaviours. Formerly from Michigan in the United States, I am absolutely delighted to say that she now calls Perth her home; will you please give a warm welcome to Lilly Andaman."

With the crowd's applause echoing through the vast hall, Lilly moved towards the podium and stood looking out over the sea of faces before her. Drawing in a deep breath to calm her nerves, she briefly looked towards Mitch sitting with Grace on his lap and Zac and Zahera next to him. As Mitch beamed a smile back to her and nodded his head in encouragement, Lilly began.

"Thank you, Madam Chancellor, and good afternoon ladies and gentlemen.
I remember as a child growing up in Empire, Michigan, my intense fascination with history and fantasies of time travel. My father had built a tree house in our backyard for my sister and me to play in, and from the heights of that tree house I could see for miles over Lake Michigan. However, that tree house to me was something far more. I used to pretend it was a time machine and it could take me back to all those momentous events in history so I could be a part of it. I would close my eyes and imagine what it would be like to be present and bear witness to history. Such was

my immense fascination with this ideal that I later enrolled in College to become a history teacher. I wanted to share all of the wonders of how those events of the past had transformed and created the present day being experienced by every child sitting in that classroom."

"However, with those child-like musings of the past I was always left with a quandary; if I had such a magic ability of time travel, whereby I could intervene and change a past event, would I? What if I was at the helm of the *Titanic* and could change the navigated course by one degree? What if I stood upon the grassy knoll and blocked the view of a gunman, aimed and ready to fire at the motorcade carrying John F. Kennedy? What if a simple spill of a coffee cup upon the lap of woman prevented her meeting with a man with whom she would have conceived a child, a child named Adolf Hitler? Or what if I was an air traffic controller that had the power to ground all flights on September 11th, 2001, because of inclement weather? Would I?"

"If history teaches us anything, it is the power of hindsight. When individual events are surrounded by frames of reference providing a linear perspective of a past, present and future, then our judgements reign supreme. We get to clearly see the 'big picture' of where those events ultimately led to and the reality we experience as our present moment. Hindsight provides us with a twenty-twenty vision of clearly seeing a deeper interconnectedness between events and circumstances that at the time remain unforeseen and invisible. It is only through the transcendence of time that the unknown becomes known, the invisible made visible. When we seek to remove in isolation any event of history and place our judgements upon it, then as human beings we are prone to condemnation. Our natural predisposition to condemn surely arises from our attachment to measure such historic events within the boundaries of human suffering and adversity. Such measurement even extends to our own personal lives, the quality of which seems to be governed and directed towards ensuring preservation from conflict and hardship; the eternal pursuit of happiness and liberty drives our inner most being."

"As parents we may often be asked what do we aspire for our children, what are our hopes for their future? The common answer would be a desire for their success and happiness, to live a long and fruitful life. In essence we wish for them to be free of our own experiences, which may have brought upon us suffering and discontent. Our parenthood, in many respects, is this guardianship of our children along a path that we believe will achieve this end. Wisdom is seldom allowed to flourish through self-experience, but rather through avoidance and detours from our perceptions of what we may personally consider harmful or detrimental experiences of life."

"Yet maybe as a parent, a community or nation, we should reconsider a new way of perceiving the experience of cataclysms, catastrophes and personal dramas seen only through the eyes of suffering. Perhaps the twenty-twenty vision of hindsight could be brought to bear within the moment of our deepest despairs and sorrows, a certain trust and faith in what is yet unseen, yet unknown, yet to unfold. Maybe the ultimate paradox of life is that from the bended knee of our burdens weighing heavily upon our backs, we will see with greater vision what was before unseen from loftier heights. Perhaps from the valleys of our deepest despair, the journey and path to the mountain of self-discovery is more clearly revealed and seen rising before us. What if seeded within the darkness of emotional turmoil and turbulence, lay hidden a light that would illuminate and shine a path to the inner sanctums of our freedom and truth. For there is no greater shackle on our inherent right to freedom and truth than one imposed by that of ignorance."

"As human beings we seem to revere and treasure those qualities and aspects of our lives only when we stand on the precipice of loss. The value of some object or quality, whether it is our health, status, wealth, or loved ones seem to expand in proportion to the potential of it being taken away from us. Aversion to loss seems to rally within us a drive or urge towards preservation or rescue from the perception of pain and suffering we believe that loss will deliver. Maybe Mother Nature in her sublimeness knew it would take enormous jeopardies and crises to push a human being towards a revelation of their human potential; to rally them from a sleeping ignorance, towards an awakened state in search of self-knowledge and their own divinity."

"Whether it is personal or human history, it is this perception of loss through adversity and challenge that has rallied the individual and the collective in the search of peace and harmony, both within and without. For truth and freedom seem to lie dormant and inert, awaiting patiently the seeker to whom its revelation would be made. As a historian, one would look back at the last millennium and see that mankind's search for meaning and purpose had been severely hampered by access to historical records, distortion of historical events and suppression of information. Our modern day century was unprecedented in manipulating information access through media censorship and bias, misreporting, corporate interests, economic blackmail and theological dogma. As Johann Van Goethe claimed in the eighteenth century:

'None are more hopelessly enslaved
than those who falsely believe they are free'.

"If the past millennium was suppression and ignorance, then surely the word that defines our last decade would be that of *disclosure*. December 21st, 2012 was prophesised by many as the end time of civilisation. The timely advantage of hindsight has again revealed that in fact this date proved to be a pivotal point in human history, a massive change and tipping point in mankind's evolution. The interconnectedness of the World Wide Web above the surface reflected the deeper interconnectedness of the human spirit below the surface. Knowledge that was previously suppressed and inaccessible to the multitudes, bubbled up through the Internet and literally changed the course of history. Science was at last freed from corporate interference and domination, to freely venture without hindrance, into a deeper exploration of consciousness and the true nature of our reality."

"The draconian age, fuelled by a 'survival of the fittest' mentality, dragged the human existence into one of perpetual war with itself, fuelled by a perception of scarcity and limited access to recourses for survival. Superstition, fear and mistrust brought human civilisation to the brink of extinction. The theories and conclusions of a free science have now proven this age-old perception of man's separateness and independent existence from nature is inconsistent with the new scientific paradigm of consciousness. We now know that at the fundamental, primary level of existence there exists an intelligent creative force of energy and consciousness that connects not only mankind, but the universe itself."

"Our paradigm shift in understanding the true nature of reality in the last decade has been paralleled by the shift in the levels of consciousness of the human entity and family. As we have come to more fully understand and accept the true interconnectedness of the cosmos, we have moved beyond a fear-based and limited perception of reality. Instead, a world where creativity, intellectual understanding, freedom and compassion predominate; a world where the highest human potential is accepted as the norm rather than the exception. A Golden Age has indeed arrived."

"So, in answer to my previous question, would I change the events of history if I could? The answer seems much more obvious with the twenty-twenty vision of hindsight; no I would not. Would I change the events of my own personal history? No, I would not. When I view life from the perspective of individual, isolated events, then I am surely plunged into the depths of despair and suffering. But, when I stand back and see those same events in the light of a symbiotic and perfect act of creation, where every historic event has subtle purpose and meaning, then instead that suffering finds some place of solace and relief. They become like birthing pains; a recognition that a new wave of life is emerging from the old."

"Maybe then, as parents, when asked what do we aspire for our children, a new answer could be contemplated. Instead of seeking to protect them from hardships and adversities, rather we nurture them towards one of resilience. When we come to understand the challenges of life as leading us towards a greater opportunity to unveil the enigma and mystery of our inner truth, to reach the pinnacles of self-realisation, then those challenges are transformed into an adventure rather than one of pain and suffering. Adversities reveal opportunities to reclaim our inherent birth rite, that being an understanding of the intrinsic unity of all life and our eternal and infinite connection to the Divine Creator."

"When we come to understand this unity and live each day as a being awakened to our spiritual truth and heritage, then compassion and empathy become our new standard for conscious living. We live with an ability to rise above our own personality and share with all mankind a service towards the greater good and brotherhood of man. When our hands are banded together as one, with a common intention to serve humanity, then our lives take on a whole new meaning and purpose. When I look out upon this audience and see the new wave of enlightened minds ready to embark upon 'the road ahead', who have stood in receivership of this new, open and free knowledge of their divine birth rite, then I am reassured that the historic events of bygone days were indeed filled with relevance and purpose. If what we have deemed and labelled with words such as catastrophe and cataclysms secretly concealed man's evolutionary rise towards his divine consciousness to be shared with all, then our past history should never be desired to be interfered with or changed. Instead we should stand as grateful recipients of the many lives, past and present, who forged a new world that stands united in heart and common service in lifting the levels of human consciousness yet higher still. We truly stand on the shoulders of giants."

"When we come to view, not only our global history, but also our own personal history, with these new eyes of understanding, then every life takes on great significance and relevance. Each and every one of you, when given the gift of life, is given a blessed opportunity to record upon the pages of history. Whether it is one word, one line, one paragraph or one chapter; all become equal in value when added to the collective conscious. So in closing today, let me leave you with this thought. How do you want history to remember you? Will it record your acts of virtue, charity and grace? Who did you forgive? Who did you bestow your acts of compassion upon? Who did you inspire and uplift? Whose hand did you hold in comfort and support? In life, you may never get to see firsthand the ripples of your influence, whether they be creative or destructive, that extend far beyond what you can ever imagine. You are a powerful being within the grand cosmic family of life and history waits patiently to see what you will write."

"I would like to thank the University of Western Australia for the honour of being able to talk to you all today; it has been an absolute privilege. I wish each of you a long and prosperous journey on the road ahead, and may God bless you all. Thank you."

As Lilly made her way down the stairs of the stage, the sound of the audience's applause reverberated around the hall. Mitch stood with Grace held in his arms as they walked towards the back and out through the wooden doors to the vibrant afternoon sun outside.

On reaching the vast expanse of lawn Grace turned to Lilly and asked, "Can I have that ice-cream now Mummy? I was a good girl for Daddy."

Lilly laughed and replied, "Yes, sweetheart, we can go and get that ice-cream now."

Filled with excitement, Grace ran off ahead, chasing the flock of seagulls that had been nestled peacefully on the lawn. Lilly laughed as Mitch took off in pursuit of their little girl.

As she slowly walked back towards the car park, Lilly's awareness was drawn to a figure of a man sitting on the ground under the huge Moreton Bay fig tree. After a few moments, she came to recognise the familiar figure of the prophet. As Lilly smiled and gave him a subtle wave, his familiar voice fired into her mind,
"Well done my love…. well done…. I love you very much, you know."

ACKNOWLEDGMENTS

It is often said that when the student is ready the teacher appears. For myself, it was in the winter of 2012 that my teacher, the prophet, made himself known in my life. For a soul who had been driven to the depths of despair and depression, the arrival of my hierophant at long last heralded in a new dawning in my life. It was the prophet who taught me to dream the dream; to start all over again when it seemed I had lost everything. For not only did he share with me a universal library of knowledge, but the passion and revelation that life is far more extraordinary that I ever knew. This book is the manifestation of the prophet's inspiration and teachings that unveiled and created my new life, from the ashes of the old. It is with much love and eternal gratitude that I give thanks to you, my teacher, 'the prophet.'

I would also like to thank the wonderful Rachel Hoare from Perth WA for her brilliant editing and assistance with bringing the book to publishing standard

www.ingramcontent.com/pod-product-compliance
Lightning Source LLC
Chambersburg PA
CBHW051133020726
47501CB00005B/1488